Blinding light greeted Weiss when he swung the door open and stepped outside. As his eyes adjusted, he detected the swirl of dry wind all around him, and the buzzing sound seemed to grow louder by the moment. Eventually his vision cleared, and he saw that he'd just emerged from a huge factory in the middle of a vast desert.

Where the hell am I?

But it wasn't his geographical location that was of immediate concern. It was the fact that he was in the direct line of flight of a crop duster, which had been buzzing through the sky overhead and was now hurtling lower and lower, aiming its front propeller directly at him. He turned and fled, running as fast as he could through the loose sand, and diving to the ground just in time to avoid being turned into propeller grist.

This seemed a lot more elegant when Cary Grant was doing it, Weiss thought as he struggled to his feet, preparing to flee once again as the crop duster circled around for another pass.

Also available from

SIMON SPOTLIGHT ENTERTAINMENT

ALIAS™

TWO OF A KIND?

FAINA

COLLATERAL DAMAGE

REPLACED

THE ROAD NOT TAKEN

VIGILANCE

STRATEGIC RESERVE

ONCE LOST

NAMESAKES

ALIAS™

THE
APO™
SERIES

OLD FRIENDS

BY STEVEN HANNA

An original novel based on the
hit TV series created by J. J. Abrams

SSE
SIMON SPOTLIGHT ENTERTAINMENT
New York London Toronto Sydney

SSE

SIMON SPOTLIGHT ENTERTAINMENT
An imprint of Simon & Schuster
1230 Avenue of the Americas, New York, New York 10020

Manufactured in the United States of America
First Edition 10 9 8 7 6 5 4 3 2 1
Library of Congress Control Number 2006923101
ISBN-13: 978-1-4169-2443-2
ISBN-10: 1-4169-2443-4

CHAPTER 1

NEW ORLEANS
SIX YEARS AGO

A high-pitched squeal of female laughter contrasted sharply with the low grinding of ineptly shifted gears. The rental car lurched forward, and for a moment it seemed like it was about to burst into a determined spurt of speed before it shuddered pathetically to a stop, its transmission emitting a pained groan as the driver slumped giggling over the steering wheel.

"You have to be the worst driver I've ever seen!" Sydney Bristow marveled, leaning back in the passenger seat. She was amazed that the airbags hadn't been triggered by that last abrupt stop. "You do understand the point is to make the car go forward, right?"

Keiko Terajima turned her head slightly and peered out at Sydney from the crook of her elbow. Her eyes were all that Sydney could see, and they seemed to be smiling. "You're going to be mad," Keiko began, feigning embarrassment, "but could you remind me which one's the clutch again? They shouldn't put it so close to the other pedals. It makes everything more confusing."

Sydney sighed a very loud sigh, playing the part of the exasperated driving instructor even though she was having more fun than she'd had in a long time. Keiko was in one of her graduate classes at UCLA, and they'd bonded when a late-night study session in the library turned into a caffeine-fueled who-likes-who gossip exchange that still hadn't ended at sunrise. They both botched the next day's exam, but they'd been close ever since, and for Sydney it was a real pleasure to have a school pal. Her best friend would always be Francie, of course, but she couldn't talk to Francie about how bad the critical essay was that she had to read for Lit. 47, or about what a kiss-up that tattooed girl had been in lecture the other day. And Keiko never asked questions about Sydney's job at Credit Dauphine—to Keiko, it was just the way Sydney was paying for tuition, an uninteresting means to an end—which meant that Sydney never had to lie to her. There were advantages to having more casual friends when one was leading a double life.

And now here they were in New Orleans, where they were both giving papers at the national meeting of the Scholars of American Literature. The SAL conference was a welcome departure for Sydney from the world of shadowy intrigue and muscle-straining roundhouse kicks. Ever since she'd learned that SD-6, the organization she worked for, was in fact not at all a government agency but a rogue operation headed by the loathsome Arvin Sloane, her life as a spy had been even more of a drain on her mental energies. Playing the part of a loyal SD-6 agent while actually working for the CIA under the stewardship of an attractive handler named Michael Vaughn was taking its toll on her ability to concentrate in her classes, and getting away for a few days to a gorgeous Southern city to give a paper on F. Scott Fitzgerald was exactly the break from spying that she needed. It was nice to pretend, if only for a little while, that she was just a typical grad student, nothing more. Sydney had been overjoyed to hear that Keiko was attending the conference as well, and since Keiko had been in the market for a new car and was considering a model that only came in stick shift, they figured taking Sydney's rental car out for a spin would be a perfect opportunity for Keiko to practice. "I warn you, I'm a newbie when it comes to driving stick," Keiko had said, and she hadn't been kidding. Keiko was really putting this poor little jalopy through its paces. If Sydney hadn't paid for rental insurance, she would actually be a little worried, but as it was, every grinding lurch of their rented red coupe was positively hilarious.

"It was really morbid of you, Sydney, to suggest we come out to this old cemetery for me to practice," laughed Keiko as she gamely turned the key in the ignition once again. "I mean, by the time I'm through with it, this car is going to be ready for a funeral of its own."

"I wanted someplace quiet and deserted, and with some hills so you could get used to the other gears. But I don't think you're going to get out of first." Keiko gave it too much gas and came to a sudden stop. Sydney felt her stomach rise a little as she was thrown back into the seat. She remembered the time she'd been in an airplane whose wings were sheared off by two skyscrapers. She'd crashed the aircraft into the raging water off a Caribbean island, using a jacket she'd stripped off a K-Directorate flunkie for a braking parachute. And yet Keiko's driving struck her as a pretty rough ride. Perhaps Keiko shouldn't be investing in an expensive new car—that money might be better spent on a million bus tokens. *The city of Los Angeles would be a safer place without Keiko Terajima on its streets,* Sydney thought to herself, then giggled. Keiko smiled too, letting the contagious laughing fit overcome her as well.

For this one weekend in New Orleans, Sydney's greatest fear would be that her grad school friend might flood the engine of her rental car. What a welcome change from worrying about the security of the world!

A man knelt before a mausoleum, hands folded in his lap, head bowed. He did not pray. Praying wasn't really his style. His unclosed eyes, ever alert, passed quickly over the epitaph on the grave, which apparently contained a "loyal soldier in the army of

Andrew Jackson." This soldier's bones had been resting here, a few feet away, for close to two hundred years. That struck the man as an awfully long time to have been dead.

The man had been responsible for the laying to rest of many bones, much more recently than the nineteenth century, in wars much more brutal and much more covert than the War of 1812. He wondered idly if the spirits of the men, women, and children he killed ever chatted with those who'd died before them. Did the soldier buried here, who probably passed on bravely in open warfare, protecting America from British invasion, sit openmouthed and stunned in the afterlife as he listened to the souls of the family of four the man had butchered last month in Boston? The man shook his head. The idea of a powwow among the souls of the dead was ridiculous. *Of course that sort of thing doesn't happen,* the man thought, putting the notion aside. *There is no afterlife. Each person I kill simply ceases to exist the moment I terminate his life. Just as I will cease to exist as well, someday.* The hint of a grin played across the man's face as he thought the words he always added when philosophical ruminations like these came to him: *Perhaps it will happen today.*

OLD FRIENDS

The knife felt heavy on his hip. Other men in his profession used guns, but he knew there was an asterisk next to his name in the Rolodexes of the rich and ruthless because he had style. *There's nothing more stylish than dispatching someone with a perfectly sharpened blade,* the man reflected as he heard yet another annoying tittering come from the abused rental car nearby. The sound grated on his ears, but it pleased him to think that his target remained so unaware that the end was near.

They want me to kill a student, he thought with a smile, picturing a meek little thing with her hair in a bun, a pencil tucked behind her ear, and spectacles perched on her plain little face. *Her skin's probably pale and pasty from endless hours poring over books in a library carrel,* he thought. *My knife will look so nice slicing through it!* This job would be a pleasure.

"I think she's starting to get the hang of it, don't you?" muttered Michael Vaughn, not really expecting a response. The noncommittal grunt that came from Jack Bristow could have been a yes or a no, or it could have been an indication that Jack thought anything Vaughn could possibly say would not be worthy of consideration. Vaughn knew Jack didn't care much for him. *He probably thinks I have inappropriate feelings for his daughter, feelings that a handler shouldn't have for his charge,* Vaughn reckoned. *And he's right. I do.*

But Jack had asked him to come along. He'd found only a single line about a "New Orleans job" amid pages and pages of otherwise fairly typical terrorist chatter, but Jack had red-flagged it and funneled it to Vaughn, who quickly alerted his superiors. However, no one had deemed it a solid enough lead to merit expending manpower to investigate—Vaughn thought sometimes that the CIA underestimated what an important asset they had in Sydney Bristow—and Jack felt uncomfortable utilizing SD-6 personnel to thwart what could, for all he knew, be an operation funded by Sloane and his cohorts. Furthermore, Jack knew how much this time away from SD-6 meant to Sydney, so he didn't want to suggest she cancel her trip or ruin it by telling her to be on the lookout. Vaughn understood this. He too thought it would be nice if Sydney could go a weekend without worrying about someone trying to kill her. And he was flattered when Jack had asked him to come with him to New Orleans and keep covert surveillance on Sydney. "I need more eyes," Jack had said flatly. Vaughn had had to suppress a smile. "I've got two," he'd said. If Jack had had to suppress a grin in return, he showed no sign of it.

Now the two men were perched side by side behind a rather ugly-looking angel monument on a crest above the road where Sydney and her friend were chugging along in a red Ford Focus. Jack and Vaughn's dark blue sedan was parked nearby, and they peered intently through binoculars, scanning the area for signs of trouble. The cemetery was beautiful, overgrown with thick Southern foliage that hung down wetly over peacefully winding roads and paths. Green and gorgeous, it was the kind of place where, one imagined, the dead slept particularly well.

Vaughn's task was to scan the perimeter, but so far he'd spotted nothing. Occasionally tourists would admire the metalwork of the cemetery gates, and now and then someone would stroll through and meander among the graves, taking a rubbing or pausing to reflect upon a weathered monument. But Vaughn had detected nothing that set off alarm bells. It was possible that the CIA higher-ups were right, and nothing was going to happen.

"Maybe the bad guys are taking the day off," he whispered to Jack, receiving the same harrumph in response. "So do you think—"

Before Vaughn could finish his sentence, Jack was gone. He'd leaped to his feet, moving quickly and purposefully down the hill at a brisk clip, somehow traveling at top speed without seeming like he was expending an ounce of energy to do so. Under other circumstances, Vaughn might have taken a moment to admire Jack's cool professionalism. Instead, he sprang up and bolted after Sydney's father.

"That's it, that's it, that's it!" Sydney cried, opening the passenger-side door and jumping out onto the smooth gravel of the road. "I think I'm safer outside the car. It's a good thing you're a better Faulkner scholar than you are a driver!"

"Oh, come on!" protested Keiko with a smile, brushing her long black hair back out of her face to peer out the rolled-down passenger window. "I'm gonna figure it out. I just need to keep trying. And anyway, I can't get this thing going fast enough to really crash! It's not like your life's in any danger."

"Keiko, every one of these dead people is lying there thinking they're going to have some new neighbors just as soon as you get on the road! I've got too much to live for, and I don't plan on . . ." Sydney trailed off. Keiko sparred back, chirping something about how she'd like to see Sydney do better, but Sydney didn't hear a word of it. She'd caught sight of something on the far side of the car, behind Keiko, and she was momentarily frozen in place. But it only took a moment before she snapped into action. Moving swiftly around the car, she opened the driver's-side door and pushed Keiko over into the passenger seat. Keiko protested laughingly.

"I was kidding!" Keiko insisted, but Sydney was already pulling the door shut and starting up the car. "Seriously, is the lesson over already?"

It's just getting started, Sydney thought. "Time to learn by watching for a bit, Keiko," Sydney said, trying to sound cheerful as she sped away and out of the cemetery, leaving the man her father was about to pummel behind them.

All he'd seen was the gleam of a knife, but that was enough. Jack had moved entirely on reflex. He hadn't said a word to Vaughn before leaping to his feet, because Vaughn wasn't worth wasting any attention on. Vaughn had already failed to recognize the threat when the man with the knife had entered the cemetery, and if he wasn't keeping his eyes open, then what had been the point of bringing him along? *This boy thinks he's worthy of my daughter,* Jack thought, *but he's not even worthy of being a government agent.* The thought disappeared as quickly as it had come. Jack's focus did not waver. He had to stop the assassin before Sydney was hurt.

The man didn't even know what hit him. Jack moved up behind him so silently and quickly that his fist connected with the man's head and decked him in what felt like a continuous motion that began at the top of the hill and ended at the bottom. With practiced swiftness Jack removed the knife from the man's grip and tossed it aside, then pinned the man down, bending his arm back until he could feel that familiar ready-to-snap stiffness in the shoulder. "Who are you working for?" Jack asked tersely, hearing a soft crunch as he pressed the man's cheek into gravel.

"I don't know," the man seethed, feeling his

tendons stretch like taffy. "Some college kid pissed at his TA, I guess. Who else would want to off a grad student?"

"That student," hissed Jack, lifting the man and flipping him over onto his back, "happens to be my daughter." It was as this last word escaped his lips that Jack's gaze locked onto the man's eyes. The glimmer he was met with would have been recognizable even if the eyes themselves hadn't been familiar: The man was a consummate pro. He clearly felt no fear, and he was looking for the tiniest opening to free himself, evade his captor, and return to his mission. This single-minded dedication to pursuing a target was something Jack knew well. After all, he'd learned it from the same people as the man he was pinning down. Jack's eyes had scanned for similar opportunities countless times in the past, and he had always found one.

"I'm sorry, Jack," came Vaughn's out-of-breath voice from behind him. "I fell as I was coming down the hill. . . ."

Jack had barely turned to look at Vaughn, shifting his eyes only for a fraction of a second from those of the man in his grip, but for a highly trained assassin, it had been opening enough. Suddenly

Jack's hands were empty, and the man was gone. Jack's anger didn't manifest itself in any visible way, though his fists clenched involuntarily on empty air. A sigh of frustrated annoyance escaped his lips, and a quick look around revealed that the man had vanished. The assassin was probably mere meters away, but a man with his training could turn meters into miles in the blink of an eye. Jack pushed past Vaughn and started heading back to their car.

"Who was that, Jack?" Vaughn asked. But no answer was forthcoming. Jack was already hurrying away, once again leaving Vaughn behind.

Decades of experience in covert ops don't teach one what to think in crisis situations. They teach one what not to. Paramount among the things the man did not think as he zigzagged from tombstone to tombstone was *I should abandon the mission.* There were no circumstances, not even the fading away of consciousness that precedes death, that would have caused a seasoned veteran like him to consider failure as an option. Nor did he think, *I wonder if I'm being followed.* Even a pursuer familiar with his evasion protocols couldn't track him, so versed was he in the art of concealing his movements, and besides, he knew that any expenditure of mental energy on worry about what was behind him would reduce the amount of thought he could give to what lay ahead, namely his target. Perhaps curiously, he was so focused on carrying out the assassination he'd agreed to perform that he didn't even think about how this particular girl had protection. *Which means my job is going to get a lot more complicated.*

In fact, although professionalism dictated that he allow no stray thoughts whatsoever to crowd in upon his narrow focus, the man indulged himself with exactly two moments of personal reflection.

In the first, as he opened the door to his brown Mustang and fished for a revolver in the glove compartment, he thought to himself, *It's a terrible shame I've lost my knife. That was a fine one, one of my favorites. The whole thing will be so much messier with a bullet than it would have been with a blade. The girl might actually be disappointed that she has to die so inelegantly.*

And in the second, as he floored the gas pedal and began the cat-and-mouse game of finding his quarry on the city streets, he thought, with the most fleeting moment of regret he'd ever felt in his entire life, *If I'd known it was Jack Bristow's kid, I'd never have taken the job.*

Shift smoothly, stay calm. Scan rearview: No pursuer visible. Don't use turn signals, but turn frequently. Who could it have been? And why is Dad here? No time to consider that. Keep focus: Escape, regroup, take initiative. Don't get killed. Oh, and I need to be at Tulane in time for that meet and greet with Dr. Fraleigh. His work on Tender is the Night *really is groundbreaking, and I've heard he hates to be kept waiting.*

"You really do make it look easy, Sydney. But it's like a juggling act, isn't it? Thinking about all those different things at once?"

Oh, right. Keiko. Can't forget she's here. Slow down: She mustn't realize anything's going on. The last time someone learned something about my extracurriculars, he wound up dead in my bathtub. Danny. Gosh, I can't think about him right now. No time for crying. I have to focus, concentrate. That brown convertible two or three cars back—it's made the same last three turns I have. Check it: Slow a little, cut the space, then make an abrupt left. Will he follow? No! Drove right on by. Either he's not the guy, or he's too much of a pro to give himself away like that. Mental note: brown sports car.

"But you juggle it all so well! The way you work your feet in time with the gearshift, it's like a little ballet you're performing there, Syd. And here I thought your only skills were in close readings and poststructuralist analysis!"

I have to make a joke back. She can't catch on that something's amiss.

"Uh, well, you know . . . you seemed so intent on deconstructing my rental car, Keiko, I felt like I had to step in. . . ."

Laughter. She's being charitable, chuckling even at bad jokes like that one. That's good. Make Keiko laugh, keep her happy, don't let her—wait! That was a flash of brown in the side mirror, wasn't it? If it comes to it, what do I have in the way of defense? Scan the car interior, assess the surroundings. Book bags, full of purchases from that used bookstore this morning. Why didn't we get more hardcovers, besides those first editions Keiko bought? They'd be more useful in hand-to-hand combat. What else do I have? An umbrella, which has possibilities. Those spirit beads that Keiko, uh, "earned" on Bourbon Street last night might make a decent garrote. And there's always my laptop, which could easily crush a skull, but it's got all my notes from the entire semester. . . .

"Suddenly you seem so tense, Sydney. What, did it finally occur to you that we actually have to get up in front of that crowd today and give our talks? I get a little antsy before public speaking too, but you're gonna be great. You'll slay 'em, Syd. Seriously."

I can't let her catch me biting my lip. I have to put her at ease. Force a little giggle in response or something, keep the atmosphere in here light. But that definitely is the same brown Mustang. Well, it's time to face the hard truth.

I'm probably going to be late for the meet and greet.

As Jack weaved his blue Taurus delicately through traffic, he tried to remember when he had last seen Roger.

Time and regret had obscured many of the details of his covert ops days, and efforts to reclaim those memories by combing through old personnel files would, he knew, be stymied by the thick layers of black ink that had been applied years before, when certain activities of his had been deemed classified.

The two men had trained together, spied together, fought and nearly died together. One particularly ugly mission in Venezuela decades earlier had ended with Jack and Roger holed up, just the two of them, in a secluded cabin for more than two weeks, detoxing in tandem from a bad batch of drugs they'd been injected with by jagged-toothed captors just before a lucky break allowed them to escape through a carelessly unlatched laundry chute. Jack had nearly gone insane by the time the drugs worked their way out of his system, but Roger had crossed that line and, some might say, never quite come back. Jack could still remember lying on the floor, hallucinating. God only knows what Roger had thought he was seeing at the time, or if he ever realized that whatever it was wasn't real. Both of them had slashed furiously at thin air with razor-sharp machetes, and pummeled the empty floor with cut-up and bruised fists, and fired more than a few bullets into the walls, aiming their pistols at imaginary creatures. It was a miracle they hadn't killed each other.

Officially speaking, however, those two weeks had never happened. The black ink had seen to it that they were erased. Officially speaking, Roger did not even exist. His loyalty, after those grueling weeks in South America, had begun to wobble like a loose wheel on a shopping cart, and people in high positions had decided that Roger himself would be blackmarkered away. Jack had never expected to see him again, but here he was, his brown car circling Sydney's red one, and he was definitely real.

Setting his jaw with determination, Jack nosed forward through a few slow-moving vehicles. The tourists, cruising casually and pointing with excitement at various historical landmarks in the French Quarter, did not realize the life-and-death pas de deux that was taking place on the streets between the blue and the brown cars. Even the occupants of the red Focus the two men were dancing around couldn't possibly know the years of history that were informing the dance.

As he drove, Jack found himself thinking that he couldn't look down on Roger's becoming a hired assassin. For most of their careers, the only difference between Jack and Roger had been that the money that paid them had originated in different banks. *Are we really so far apart, even now?* Jack wondered uneasily. His lip twitched apprehensively.

Sadly, it seemed unlikely that today would end with the two of them talking over old times in a darkened bar down on Decatur Street. He wasn't the sort to indulge in these kinds of feelings, but truth be told, given a couple of Scotches and a fellow traveler down memory lane, Jack could probably find it in himself to enjoy, in his own way, the company of an old friend.

He'd identified Roger's car. There were few tailing patterns that allowed you to follow one car while remaining undetected by a second whose driver was aware of your pursuit, and although Roger was shadowing Sydney and Keiko with considerable skill, he'd shown his hand on St. Charles Avenue. Jack had lost track of him as they'd passed Canal and entered the Quarter, but as long as Jack stuck close to Sydney, he didn't have to find Roger. Roger would eventually find them. *I could flush him out if we weren't in such a crowded area,* Jack thought, gritting his teeth, *but there's no way to draw him away from Sydney.* Given the relative safety of broad daylight, Sydney was wise to be sticking to the crowded streets of the city's tourist sector, though Jack silently disapproved of her turn south toward the waterfront.

"Hey, J.B.!" came an unexpected shout from nearby. Idling at a stoplight with Sydney stopped three car lengths ahead in traffic, Jack snapped his gaze away from Sydney's car and turned to look to his side, where Roger had pulled up beside him undetected. Roger had a bright, unworried smile on his face. "I'm gonna ask you to back off, buddy. There's work to be done." Jack tensed for a moment as he thought Roger was pulling a gun, but instead Roger's hand lifted to his lips: He was simply lighting a cigarette.

"Maybe I didn't make it clear, Roger, but that's my daughter. You're not going to touch her."

"That's your daughter? Doesn't look a bit like you. Plus I wouldn't have pegged the child of a Bristow for a bookworm, my man. She must be into some serious rebelling-against-Daddy."

Jack drew in a deep breath. "Turn your car around and drive away. If you don't, I'm going to have to—"

"It's a job, Jack," Roger intoned sharply, sounding suddenly tired of talking. The cigarette smoke flowed out of his mouth as he frowned. "I took it, now it has to be done. It's a shame your progeny doesn't have more fans in high places, or the job would never have been ordered. I admit, in retrospect, I wish I'd taken that other gig knifing some suit in Stockholm instead, but what's done's, you know . . . it's done."

A loud honk sounded behind them. Roger's stare didn't move from Jack's.

"Light's green, Jack."

"Drive away. Don't move an inch closer to her."

Two more honks. Roger eyed Jack warily. "I answer to people, J.B., and they want this done. I gave my word it would be. You'd do the same thing in my—"

"I would never harm your child, Roger," Jack interrupted. "No matter who ordered the hit. No matter what justification I had."

Roger's head tilted to one side. His eyes flitted forward to the stoplight. It had turned yellow. Two horns blared now, one of them in a long, sustained bleat. Then Roger laughed, a big, jovial bellow, and he pressed the gas pedal hard. His sports car sped out into the intersection long after the light had gone red, and cars screeched around him as he sped to the other side of the street. Jack gunned the gas as well and tore off after his daughter and the man bent on killing her.

I take it back, he thought grimly. *We are pretty far apart.*

* * *

When Keiko screamed, Sydney jammed on the brakes reflexively and reached over to see where her friend had been hit. After Danny's death, she'd sworn to herself that her work would never affect the people she cared about again, much less hurt them, and the idea that her carelessness in coming to New Orleans and letting her guard down had put Keiko in jeopardy made her feel terrible. Now she searched for the wound frantically, hoping to staunch the bleeding before it was too late. She was not going to let Keiko die.

"Whoa there, Bristow! Quit pawing me!" Keiko shouted, obviously unhurt and a bit shocked at Sydney's familiarity. "I'm not that kind of girl!" Sydney pulled her hands back, confused. "I just felt your phone ringing from somewhere on the floor, and it startled me. What's with you?"

Sydney had set her cell on vibrate, and Keiko must have felt the telltale whirr. As Sydney stammered an apology for the well-intentioned but unexplainable manhandling, Keiko shrugged the moment off and bent down to rummage for the phone among all the packages and bags at her feet. "Just leave it, K," Sydney said, relief flooding over her until, through the passenger window suddenly revealed by Keiko's lowering her head, she saw the grim face of a man staring at her from the next car. He exhaled a long plume of smoke that curled menacingly in the heavy New Orleans air.

Sydney accelerated quickly, and Keiko was thrown back in the seat, surprised that they weren't done experimenting with the car's stop-and-start limits today. "Got it!" she cried, holding Sydney's phone up in triumph.

"Whoever it is," Sydney said as she made a sudden turn, "I'll call back later."

"Ooh, no! It's that cute reporter friend of yours!" Keiko exclaimed, peering at the caller ID in the phone's front window. "I'm gonna answer it."

"No, not now . . ." Sydney began, but Keiko had already snapped the phone open and begun chattering away.

"Hello?" she said playfully. "No, it's not Sydney, silly! Well, why don't you guess who it is?" Sydney couldn't help shaking her head a little. Keiko was an inveterate flirt, and Sydney never ceased to be amazed by the cooing girlishness she fell into whenever she spoke to a member of the opposite sex. Generally speaking, she'd found it best to keep Keiko away from her male friends.

"No, guess again," Keiko said sweetly, before suddenly turning indignant. "Absolutely not! Why would you guess her? I don't sound a thing like her!"

Sydney's fingers tensed on the wheel as she glimpsed brown metal at the head of a street she was turning down, then relaxed as she realized it was just another similarly shaded sedan. *Keiko's distracted. That's good. Now focus on getting her to safety.*

"You're the investigative journalist. You should be good at asking questions and getting people to reveal their true identities. Isn't that what you do for a living?" There was a pause, during which Keiko began to giggle. "Well, that doesn't seem like a very perceptive question, but yes, I do have long black hair and a stunning smile. See, I knew you knew who it was all along! You should have been calling me anyway, 'cause Sydney's not the only one giving a paper today. I need to be wished good luck too."

A small explosion in the brick wall next to their car signaled a silenced bullet missing its target, but Sydney, used to the sound, barely flinched. The brown car's tires screeched as it fell into line close behind hers. Her eyes moved over to Keiko as she spun the wheel sharply, hoping her friend hadn't noticed the gunshot or the uptick in their speed as Sydney fled. Sure enough, she hadn't: Keiko just hunched down in the seat a little, plugging her left ear with a finger as she raised her voice to be heard.

"No, we're just in a loud part of town, I guess. So tell me what you're working on these days!"

Clenching her teeth nervously, Sydney spun around a corner and saw an opportunity. Pulling into a tiny Starbucks parking lot, she tucked her car into a handicapped space for a moment. She watched with satisfaction as the brown Mustang sped past behind her.

"You're searching for a mystery woman? How very cloak-and-dagger of you!" Keiko was saying, before putting her hand over the receiver and whispering, "Stopping for coffee? Great idea. I'll take, like, a double latte with—"

"Changed my mind," faked Sydney, pulling out and heading back the way they'd come. "We really ought to get to the conference." Keiko just shrugged, the look in her eyes suggesting that they'd both regret it later on when the academic droning reached full swing.

"No, no, I'm listening," Keiko insisted, turning back to her phone conversation. "Well, I could give you to Sydney, but she's driving, and you know what they say about driving while using a cell phone. Very unsafe. You wouldn't want to put us in any danger, would you?" She flashed a conspiratorial smile at Sydney, and Sydney mustered a false chuckle in response.

The engine growled as Sydney ran up the rpm's before making a dash across a relatively uncrowded intersection. She was beginning to regret her turn south, which boxed her in against the Mississippi. It had made sense at the time to turn the assassin away from the conference up north, since that was where she planned on ending up, but her options were limited down here, with so little ground to her left.

"No, but I'll tell you what I really want to know," tittered Keiko. "I want to know how available you are. 'Cause I have some ladies lined up for you, mister, if you're not too hung up on that Francie." A moment passed, and then Keiko laughed, maybe even a little shrilly. "I have a sense for these things, that's how! What's that? No way. It'll never last with Charlie. Have you met the guy? Between you and me, I think he may bat for a different team, if you know what I mean. But even if that wasn't the case, you should write her off anyway, because I know a pretty little thing in the English department who would be perfect for you." She nudged Sydney playfully, and Sydney winced at this overt example of Keiko's unflagging matchmaking.

"Oh!" Keiko said, sitting up sharply as she remembered something. "Come to think of it, I actually know two gorgeous girls there! Because Sydney's almost as perfect for you as I would be!" Pleased with her little joke, Keiko fell into laughter, then composed herself and said sternly into the phone, "No, seriously, though, I'm going to take down your number and call you when a promising candidate comes up. Give me a minute to find something to write with. . . ."

Keiko bent down to search for a pen and paper in her purse. Sydney stopped suddenly to avoid colliding with a delivery truck that barreled out in front of her. She turned to look through the open passenger window, and once again she gasped in terror at what she saw: A man was staring at her down the barrel of a gun. And the man's face belonged to her father.

Jack must have recognized the fear in Sydney's expression as their eyes locked, because he furrowed his brow sternly. She snapped her head around, realizing his aim was locked on something behind her, and through the open driver's-side window she saw another gun, this one trained on her by Roger. Her mouth fell open in astonishment as she bent in two, falling over Keiko protectively.

Almost inaudible over her head, the double ping of two silenced bullets sliced through the air, followed by the piercing, sustained sound of a car horn.

Vaughn had felt like an idiot flagging down a kid on the deserted road outside the cemetery and flashing his CIA ID. He could barely believe the words were actually coming out of his mouth as he'd barked out, "I'm a government agent! I need to confiscate your scooter!" The kid, understandably, had laughed in his face.

Adjusting his baseball cap and crossing his arms defiantly over the scooter's handlebars, the kid peered at the ID card a moment before laughing at the sight of it. "That ain't no gov'ment badge!" he'd insisted. "I could make a better one of those on my computer at home!"

"No, you couldn't," Vaughn had said with forced patience, "unless your computer was the size of a room, and your home was a top secret facility in Langley, Virginia."

"Don't even look like you."

"It's an old picture. Look, I misspoke a minute ago when I said I was going to 'confiscate' the scooter. What I really need to do is borrow it."

The kid had pursed his lips, relishing having the upper hand. "I tell you what, old man. You and me, we can work somethin' out, but ain't no 'borrow' in Lou'siana. You'd best talk barter-and-trade if you want this ride."

The kid drove a hard bargain! Vaughn eventually had to empty his pockets, offering up three hundred dollars in government "walkaround" money, the New Orleans Brass keychain he'd picked up on a whim at the airport, and a pen that he hoped the kid would never figure out was also a laser. He'd managed to hold on to his digital camera and his wristwatch, but the kid had deemed it a pretty fair trade. "Heck, I stole that scooter anyway," the kid had gloated as he sprinted away. Vaughn had shrugged and set off to track Jack's movements using the pulse reader on his watch.

Now, astride a scooter more suited to someone half his size and half his age, Vaughn careened around a corner with one foot thrust out to the side to steady himself, and as he turned, the line of three cars came into sight before him: brown, red, and blue. He skidded to a halt mere feet away, just in time to hear the distinctive sounds of two silenced bullets being fired, and then he watched Sydney sit up in the red car and speed away, the squeal of her tires masked by the blaring of a car horn. Overwhelmed with relief at the sight of Sydney, unhurt, Vaughn exhaled all the tension from his body.

He hadn't even realized he'd been holding his breath.

Roger had slithered silently up beside his quarry. *Now I've got you, schoolgirl*, he'd thought, aiming his pistol carefully, centering his sights on the girl he now knew was his old partner's daughter. The girl's youth and warmth struck him as a stark contrast to the hard steel he knew well from all those years at Jack Bristow's side. *Must take after her mother*, he'd thought to himself with a chuckle.

But then she'd disappeared, ducking down in the seat for some reason, and he'd decided to wait a moment for her to sit back up so he'd have a cleaner shot. It would prove to be the worst decision he'd ever made, and also the last. His eyes took an instant to refocus on the car beyond the girl's, but when they did, he saw the face of his old partner glaring at him coldly. For an instant seeing another man with a gun—another older man, another old soldier—Roger had fancied that he was looking into a mirror. It wasn't the first time he'd ever thought about how he and Jack were almost the same.

Even after a lapse of several decades, two people who have worked together under the intense and frostily intimate conditions of covert ops retain the ability to communicate through the merest looks and glances. Their stares locked on each other, Roger and Jack had just enough time for a brief, silent conversation before the bullets were fired.

Has it come to this? was the question Roger asked with his eyes as he pulled the trigger.

Jack could tell Sydney had no idea Roger was right beside her, with a gun aimed at her head. But his expression had conveyed to her the urgency of the moment, and she'd spun and then dropped down out of sight. *Good girl*, thought Jack, grateful that his daughter had such solid instincts. *Takes after her mother*, he thought to himself with some satisfaction.

But then he was staring into the face of his old partner, a man who knew him better than just about anyone on the planet. It was disquieting to see, in another man's eyes, a determination equal to his own, and for an instant Jack was stunned to consider that Roger's single-minded dedication to snuffing out Sydney's life was the twisted foil of his own unwavering certainty that he would do anything—break any law, cross any line—in order to save his daughter. *Maybe we're not that far apart after all*, Jack thought grimly.

Roger's question, to someone who knew him as well as Jack did, was as clarion-clear as if it had been spoken aloud. *Indeed it has*, Jack responded wordlessly, *and I'm very sorry, old friend.* With that, he too fired his gun.

Sydney was speeding away, nervously checking the rearview mirror. Behind her, growing smaller as she drove, she saw her father step out of his Taurus as another man approached him. *Is that Vaughn?* she wondered, feeling a little flutter in her heart as she recognized the familiar figure of her handler. *He's here too? Is the entire spy world vacationing on the Gulf Coast this week?*

"What's that?" Struggling to be heard over the loud, sustained car horn, Keiko was almost shouting into the phone as she straightened up in her seat. "No, that's just somebody laying on his horn somewhere behind us. I don't know what's up with New Orleans drivers. They're so rude! Now, okay, I've got a pen, let's get that number. This'll be really useful, because honestly, don't you have a sister? I have somebody in mind for her, too. There's this cute guy in the East Asian Studies Department. . . ."

Sydney could detect from her father's gait as he walked over to the brown Mustang that the danger had passed. She closed her eyes a moment, breathing a sigh of relief, driving slower than she had all afternoon now that she knew Keiko was out of harm's way. Oddly enough, although none of the edging-toward-high-speed stuff earlier had attracted Keiko's attention, the dawdling seemed to bother her.

"Hey, Syd," she whispered, covering the phone receiver, "shouldn't we kind of step on it? I mean, Professor Choy recommended we hit that Kate Chopin panel at two thirty, so we'd better head over there. We've done enough pleasure cruising anyway, don't you think?"

"Oh, yeah," Sydney replied, smiling sincerely for the first time in a while. "I don't know what got into me."

Vaughn watched Jack step out of the blue sedan and glance briefly at the torn spot in its upholstered headrest. Roger's bullet had strayed mere centimeters from the mark, but Jack had moved his head aside just in time. The blood dripping onto the leather seats of the Mustang made it clear that Roger had not been so lucky.

Jack turned to watch Sydney drive away, and Vaughn could swear he detected the tiniest glimmer of relief in the way Jack then walked toward the sports car, where he leaned in the window and pulled the lifeless body of the assassin back from its slumped-over position against the steering wheel. The car horn stopped blaring, leaving the street curiously quiet. Pressing two fingers against the man's neck to confirm that he was dead left Jack's hand coated in blood, which he wiped off on the assassin's chest. Something about the way Jack then considerately adjusted the jacket on the dead man's body to straighten the lapel struck Vaughn as odd. *Why would he be concerned about the man who had just tried to kill Sydney?*

"Did you know this guy, Jack?" Vaughn asked. "The way he looked at you back at the cemetery, I thought maybe . . ."

Jack silenced him with a glare, which deteriorated into a withering look as Jack's eyes took in the cheap scooter that stood next to Vaughn. *That thing cost me three hundred bucks,* Vaughn wanted to protest, but he remained silent. A moment passed as Jack seemed to mull something over. If pressed, Vaughn might have said Jack was struggling to compose himself.

"This man hardly matters," Jack finally said. "The important thing is that Sydney is safe."

CHAPTER 2

KUALA LUMPUR
TODAY

Sydney was in trouble. But she looked fantastic.

"Oh, Miss Cervenka, how beautiful you look!" martini-toting people would exclaim, addressing her by tonight's alias and forgetting, as they marveled, all about the swank reception going on around them. Speaking in the thick accents of the Russian professor he was impersonating, Eric Weiss had approached and bellowed how "breathtaking" she looked, while Nadia Santos, who'd assumed the guise of a low-class, dishwater-blond dish-busser, had snapped her gum while collecting empties and squeaked out breathy praises of her sister's "gaw-jis-ness." Even Marcus Dixon, listening in via comms from the building's security room, couldn't resist cracking a joke about how he'd always dreamed of whispering softly into the ear of "someone who looks as fabulous as you do, Phoenix." Sydney had rolled her eyes, but otherwise she hadn't faltered once in her note-perfect assumption of the role of an exotic Eastern European supermodel. Truth be told, she liked to believe that she looked as amazing as they said. After all, she'd dolled herself up pretty nicely tonight.

Which is why she probably still looked good now. After all, someone who'd started from such a high level of glamour couldn't possibly fall to zero just because she'd changed into rather bulky and highly unfashionable APO-issue "stealth boots," so-called by Marshall because they allowed her to step over pressure-sensitive alarm spots in the floor undetected. Nor did the supermodel in a woman evaporate just because she'd been slugged twice in the stomach after being discovered snooping around an office on an otherwise deserted upper floor of the skyscraper where the party was being held. *And having a chair broken over your back by a mustachioed Malaysian goon while snapping the arm of another*

Sydney's leg seared hotly, and the water washing over it turned red.

"I've got him on cams, Phoenix," Dixon said in her ear. "He's on the seventy-third floor. Seventy-second. Seventy-first . . ."

Dispelling the pain with sheer will, Sydney pulled herself up off the floor and dove through the fire door to the stairwell at her end of the hall. Her eyes danced over the floor numbers—75, 74—as she began to race down the stairs, paralleling Kim's descent on the opposite end of the building.

"Outrigger, where's Houdini?" she heard herself asking, her voice sounding vaguely distant, as if the throbbing of her leg was walling her in and muffling the sounds around her.

"He's been delayed downstairs," Dixon replied hesitantly. Sydney could tell he was leaving out some crucial information, but she was already dealing with severe limitations on her ability to concentrate. With reluctance she wrote off the Weiss-as-cavalry idea. The floor numbers, written in dull red on the fire doors of each story, blurred past as she sped down, turning sharply on gray concrete landing after gray concrete landing. On the sixty-fourth floor her leg gave out for a moment and she spilled to the ground. She might have passed out if she hadn't heard Dixon informing her, "You're faster than him, Phoenix. Kim's passing sixty-six. Guess he's had a few too many bulgogi dinners to stay spry on his feet."

Hauling herself up and blinking repeatedly to collect herself, Sydney gripped the handrail and hurled herself over, dropping down a floor to sixty-three and then racing through the fire door into yet another nondescript, wet hallway full of offices. Her attempt to race across the hallway to cut Kim off at his stairwell failed, however, as once again her boots gave way beneath her. This time, though, she had enough forward momentum to careen across the wet floor, bruising her side as she slipped over the wet tile, arriving with a thud against the wall on the far side of the hallway. *Now I know how one of Michael's hockey pucks feels,* Sydney thought grimly as she pulled herself tenderly to her feet and waited, ear pressed to the fire door.

It took a moment, but the clatter of Kim's feet as he ran down the stairs grew louder and louder until she could tell he was on the landing above. At just the right moment, Sydney threw the door open into his path and sprang into the stairwell, grabbing Kim and tossing him against the wall. He bounced off like a tennis ball. The extra pounds may slow a man down, but they provide useful cushioning in a scuffle.

Kim roared like Godzilla as he swung at her, shoving her back out the fire door and into the wet hallway. He continued his assault with a girlish shriek that would have been comical if he hadn't been landing such a high and effective percentage of his blows. Sydney sprang stiffly to her feet mid-way down the hall. Kim saw she was stunned and began fumbling for the gun, which he'd apparently stuffed in a pocket that had grown less accessible once he was drenched.

"You okay, Phoenix?" came Dixon's voice. He obviously hadn't realized she'd been hit and was only now registering the sluggishness in her movements.

"No, not really. I'm a little off my game here," Sydney heard herself saying aloud, and Kim paused, looking up at her curiously. She shouldn't have said that. She'd given away her weakness, and a cruel smile broke over Kim's face like an evil sunrise as he began walking slowly, intently toward her. Sydney tried to take a defensive stance but found herself collapsing against a metal cabinet on the wall instead. Her hands fell against glass, searching vainly for purchase as she began to slump down to the floor. One hand clawed ineffectually at the smooth space between a bright red *F* and an *E,* while another slid right past the letters *HO.* A tiny bell rang in her head, but it sounded so far away. . . .

"Feeling a bit under the weather, my dear?" Kim mocked. "What a shame you won't be around when the rain really starts to fall."

Sydney would have liked to have fired off a snappy comeback, but none came immediately to mind. In fact, it was right about then that everything began fading to black.

"Evergreen!" Dixon barked. "What's your status? Phoenix is in urgent need of assistance!"

No response.

"Evergreen? Evergreen!" Teeth gritted in frustration, Dixon watched the grainy black-and-white image of Sydney going limp against the upper-story hallway wall, feeling helpless as Kim's looming shadow approached her in one corner of the monitor's frame. Dixon slammed his fist angrily against the security console. *Why am I cooped up down here?* he thought angrily. *I should be up there help-*

ing. I look just as good in a tux as Weiss does. . . .

But there was no time for thoughts like these. With the other two agents apparently out of the picture, it was all up to Dixon. If they'd known Kim and his security detail would be here, they would have tasked more people to the op, but as it was, Sloane had been reluctant to let even four agents go. Weiss had basically finagled a fourth spot on the plane because he and Nadia had been flirting away for weeks, and he thought it would be fun to spend a couple of days in Malaysia making puppy-dog eyes at her. *I wish the weekend could have gone better for them,* Dixon mused. *What a shame this mess had to splash cold water on the whole thing.*

Suddenly Dixon had a realization. His eyes widened thoughtfully, and the wheels in his head spun wildly as he mentally examined every centimeter of the security room's layout before springing into action. Or, more precisely, rolling into it. Pushing off with his feet, Dixon sent his wheeled chair racing backward to another console behind him, which he scanned quickly before locating what he was looking for: a tiny wheel labeled FIRE CONTROL TEMPERATURE VALVE.

Having given it a firm couple of turns, he wheeled himself back to the bank of monitors, where he could have chosen to watch Kim suddenly flinch and recoil, shivering under the now ice-cold spray of the sprinklers. But Dixon's eyes weren't on Kim. They were on the limp figure of Sydney, who jerked spasmodically when the water temperature nose-dived, and came groaningly but perceptibly back to life as the cold spray woke her up.

"Come on, Phoenix," coaxed Dixon, leading her back to consciousness over the comm. "You can do this."

Sydney didn't say anything in response, but Dixon watched her stand, getting to her feet and carrying herself more solidly than before. He knew Sydney, and the spy trade in general, well enough to recognize what was happening: Sydney was functioning on autopilot, the instincts she'd gained from years of intense training snapping into place and governing actions she was probably barely conscious of, if at all. It was rare that an agent of Sydney's caliber found herself so cornered or so injured that she had to rely on this deeply buried level of the brain, but Dixon himself had experienced it once or twice—it was the spy equivalent, he sometimes thought, of the total detachment from the senses that religious ascetics seek through meditation—and he knew that she would find it an incredible, slightly chilling thrill when she realized later that no matter how battered she might be, her training and survival instincts would remain intact at her core.

Confidently, and coldly, Sydney took advantage of Kim's moment of distraction and smashed the container on the wall, the bright red words FIRE HOSE shattering into pieces around her fists. *That's it, Syd,* Dixon thought as he watched her unfurl the hose from its box. *Give him hell.*

Dixon leaned back in his chair, eyes locked on the screen. *Sydney at her best is better than any show on TV*, he thought with satisfaction. Kim didn't even have a chance to level his gun at her before he was hit with a torrent of freezing-cold water that knocked him off his feet and off the screen, and Sydney's expressionless visage was grainily commanding on the black-and-white monitor as she subdued her would-be killer with the paralyzing spray.

But then suddenly Dixon had to lean forward, his grin melting away like a sand castle in the rain. It was tough to tell exactly what was happening from the security camera, but Kim seemed to have found an opening, lunging past Sydney and grabbing the fire hose at a spot closer to the cabinet. Two dark shadows whirled about on the screen as he used the hose to whip Sydney around, entangling her and smashing her through the door of one of the offices. Gripping the handrests of his chair with all the helplessness of a moviegoer watching a sympathetic character buy it in a slasher flick, Dixon let his mouth fall open in shock as he saw Kim springing after Sydney, disappearing into the offscreen office. Dixon began flipping switches in desperation, looking for a camera view of what was happening in there, but there were none to be found. As he slumped back in his chair, horrified and defeated, the wheels gave way and he rolled back a few inches, coming to a clanging stop against the opposite security console. Dixon clenched his jaw in anxious frustration.

She's completely on her own.

The movies—and Sydney and her coworkers had discussed this many times—represented the spying life with surprising accuracy. Sure, as Dixon would be the first to point out, they tended to gloss over all the dull evenings spies spend studying schematics or combing through computerized bank records in search of essential but decidedly uncinematic money trails. And certainly, they deemphasized the long hours of grueling physical training required to make near-superhuman feats look effortless, which was one of Vaughn's pet peeves. And few who worked in the biz would disagree with Marshall's complaints that Hollywood vastly overstated the destructive powers of laser beams fired from space. But, although Sydney personally doubted that anyone who'd ever penned a spy story had ever seen anything more exciting in real life than the morning rush at the latte line, she couldn't help admiring the things they got right.

For instance, there was the way people in spy movies get knocked out, and then you see a series of short, fuzzy shots to convey what's happening to them as they're wheeled down a hospital corridor, reassured by doctors leaning into the camera and insisting that everything's going to be fine. Sydney always wondered how many screenwriters had actually had that experience. And yet that's pretty much exactly how it goes. Things go black, and then flashes of consciousness, barely connected one to the next, parade past until you finally wake up, hopefully in a hospital room and not in the underground lair of some supervillain.

The flashes that came after Sydney blacked out in the Malaysian hallway were searingly intense, separated by terrifying stretches of blackness. Between Kim's nasty remark about "the rain" and the warmly clinical smile of the Los Angeles doctor welcoming her back with the words "You're going to be okay," Sydney's life shuffled past her like the panels in a comic book, all in vivid, tightly framed images. There was Kim's face twisted in anguish as the spray from the hose in her hands sent him reeling back away from her; the interior of a vast, windowed office looking out on the glittering skyline of Kuala Lumpur, as seen upside down from a position thrown back over a desk, with Kim throttling her as she struggled to kick free; Kim in midair, having been hurtled back toward the window after she'd used every ounce of strength to pull her legs up and send him flying away from the desk. Shards of the smashed window were still in midair all around him, and from his face it was clear he knew it was a long way down.

Sydney remembered her own fingers clawing

desperately at the office's carpeted floor as she was dragged by Kim's weight and the fire hose tangled around her legs toward the newly made hole in the glass. She recalled the terrifying moment when she found herself falling, then relief when the hose went taut and suddenly broke her fall.

A crowd of soaked, well-dressed people stood far below, evacuated from the party after the fire alarm. They were staring and pointing up at the figure of a tattered supermodel dangling from an upper-floor window.

Sydney had seen Nadia, who looked tiny from so far above, standing handcuffed and guarded by a squad of armed guards off to one side of the dripping partygoers. Next to her Weiss lay groaning in pain as he pressed a blood-soaked towel to a wound in his side. Things had obviously gone as badly downstairs as they had up here.

Finally, she recalled the view as she was hauled back into the office window by Dixon. She had looked down to see medical crews arriving, too late, to tend to the shattered body of Eddie Kim, who'd fallen to his death on the concrete below.

After that, things had gotten difficult to follow, as she was smuggled out a back door and placed on a gurney that was wheeled onto an unmarked APO plane, where she and Weiss had lain side by side cracking jokes through the sedative haze as they flew back over the Pacific. A long black space followed, after which she could see Vaughn gazing with tender concern into her eyes, but then his face had blurred in her mind into Sloane's as he coldly assessed her wounds and declared her suspended from APO activities until she'd healed.

And then there was Dr. Cothran, his long hair hanging down over his eyes, saying, "You're going to be okay." He'd explained that they'd set the broken leg, that she'd be on crutches for a month or so and a cane for a spell after that, but that otherwise there would be no lasting effects from her injuries.

"My friend," she'd croaked, "Eric Weiss?"

Dr. Cothran rolled his eyes just a little. "He woke up much more quickly than you and seems to be recovering quite well. We were all a little sick of his magic tricks, though, so we sent him over to the kids' wing to pull some quarters out of more receptive ears." Sydney mustered up a weak smile and nodded gratefully when the doctor offered to have a nurse wheel her over to see him.

The real magic happened just as she was nodding

off in the wheelchair en route. The drab hospital corridor had started to slip away, the hubbub of medical instruments and doctor-patient discussions fading to a dull drone, when a shout pierced through it all that pulled her back to consciousness more sharply than that cold water had in Kuala Lumpur.

"Sydney Bristow, is that you?" Sydney opened her eyes to find a familiar face she hadn't seen in ages smiling wanly at her from a seat in the ER waiting area. If she'd had the strength, Sydney would have stood and run to the girl and given her a big bear hug, even though the hug couldn't have been returned. The girl, sitting and holding an icepack pressed against an obviously damaged arm—*and is that a wedding ring glittering on her hand?* Sydney wondered happily—seemed delighted to see Sydney.

But Sydney was even more excited to see her old friend, and she gleefully cried out, "Keiko Terajima! Are you ever a sight for sore eyes!"

CHAPTER 3

LOS ANGELES
FOUR WEEKS LATER

"She's late." Sydney sighed into her cell. "Entertain me."

The cheerful crackling of Vaughn's laughter in Sydney's ear was a welcome sound that she had heard far too rarely lately. Since her medically imposed suspension from APO had begun, Sydney had seen Vaughn only over rushed dinners and occasional Blockbuster nights, during which they had seemed oddly distant. But those weren't the only times she felt estranged from Vaughn now that he went to work every day, leaving her to do physical therapy and reread Thomas Wolfe. She'd sometimes wondered what other couples talked about if they didn't regularly travel together to exotic locales where they pretended to be people they weren't, and now she knew the answer: A lot of time they don't talk about much of anything at all. This was just a phase, of course, and Sydney knew it would pass as soon as she climbed out of her recovering-from-injury funk. But recently she'd been falling prey to a few dark thoughts about relationships in general, and she knew it was because she had reconnected with her old grad school pal, whose own relationship with her husband was less than picture-perfect.

Spending time with Keiko again has been wonderful, Sydney thought, tapping her cane restlessly against the bench outside a trendy Chinese restaurant, twenty minutes after Keiko was supposed to have met her for lunch. In fact, she was actually kind of glad for the suspension, since she wouldn't have had the time for chats over coffee or chick flicks on the weekend if she were halfway around the world on APO business. But the way Keiko glowed perceptibly less brightly than she had when Sydney had last seen her seemed like an ominous cloud over what marriage could lead to. Sydney had learned that Keiko and her husband Franklin had started dating not long after Sydney graduated, and in the years since Sydney disappeared into full-time spying, cutting her off from her old school friends, the two of them had tied the knot and become Mr. and Mrs. Thornhill. It wasn't for her to judge, Sydney knew, but it didn't seem much to Franklin's credit that he'd insisted Keiko should be a stay-at-home spouse, or that he'd encouraged her to drop out of school before finishing her degree. Sure, Franklin apparently did okay in his lab job, and Keiko certainly didn't seem to want for money, but the sharp mind Sydney had seen on display during lively discussions on literature had definitely been dulled by the housewife life. There was something sad about the way Keiko's once-vibrant air seemed diminished, and though Keiko had never exactly been the picture of modesty, now she seemed withdrawn and often distant. The spark that had made Keiko who she was seemed to have disappeared, or at least been exiled to some hidden place deep inside. And she definitely had a bad habit of keeping Sydney waiting!

"Is this friend of yours ever on time?" Vaughn asked. "Keiko could really use a watch."

"I know I always call you when she's late, but I'm not a good thumb-twiddler."

"I beg to differ. Everything you do, you do exquisitely," Vaughn replied.

"Now, if every unwelcome phone call from me is met with flattery, you'll only get more of them. You should be meaner, and nip this impulse in the bud," Sydney teased.

"If it were possible for a call from you to be unwelcome, I'd keep that in mind."

Sydney leaned back on the bench and idly executed a quick moulinet thrust with her cane, just to see if she still had the knack. A startled passerby recoiled with a jump, and Sydney grinned, shrugging an apology in response. "So entertain me, Mr. CIA. Tell me what you're up to."

Vaughn sighed. He'd like nothing better than to do that, but it had been forbidden. "Syd, you know I can't talk business. I'm under express orders from your dad to keep you focused on getting back on your feet."

"Tell him I'm on my feet. I'll be on them all afternoon, cruising the mall for his Father's Day gift. K's a little estranged from her father and she doesn't feel right buying him something, so she's transferring the impulse to me. I don't think she'll rest until she's helped me find just the right thing, whatever that is."

"I imagine Jack's a tough guy to shop for," Vaughn said.

How right you are, Sydney thought, pursing her lips and catching a whiff of mu shu from inside the restaurant as a customer stepped out the door. "I was thinking maybe I'd get him a . . . Oh, wait a second. That's the call waiting, it's probably Keiko." Anticipating a second beep, Sydney punched a button and chirped cheerfully, "Hey, where are you? I'm starving!"

"Sitting at home," came the slightly confused reply, "watching *The Price Is Right* and gorging myself on Sun Chips. Where are you?"

"Eric!" Sydney exclaimed in surprise. "I'm sorry, I thought you were someone else."

"Who, besides you and me, Syd, is free to sit and yammer on the phone at this time of day?" Weiss asked. His voice conveyed the heaviness of too many afternoons on the couch. "Everyone else we know is working, saving the world, or at least doing something more worthwhile than watching people guess the retail price of a Sea-Doo. Which costs way more than this idiot thinks, by the way."

"The suspension won't last forever. You should enjoy it while it lasts."

"You shoulda told me that an hour ago, before I opened bag number two. These chips are not meant to be consumed in mass quantities."

"Um, listen, Eric, I have Vaughn on the—"

"This'll just take a sec, Syd. It's just, I've been thinking, and I could use your help. I'm planning to, um . . . well, to ask Nadia to move in with me. It seems like maybe it's time."

"Eric, that's fantastic! Congratulations! I'm so happy for you!"

"Well, the thing is, I'm not exactly sure she'll say yes. And I don't—"

"Of course she'll say yes! You two are great together."

"I like to think so, yeah." Weiss sounded simultaneously pleased to hear she thought so, and skeptical that she was right. "But then I remember that she's so great, and so gorgeous, and I'm sitting here wearing a sweatshirt covered in crumbs, debating whether it's somehow ethically wrong to undercut everyone before you on Contestants' Row by bidding one dollar."

"Being suspended starts to play with your head a little," Sydney argued, trying to remind herself that that was exactly what was going on with her and Vaughn. "No one should have this much free time. But Nadia will be overjoyed."

"Well, that's why I was calling. I don't want to ask and then get shot down, 'cause that would be really embarrassing, and, well . . . I thought maybe you could sort of suss things out a little, see how receptive Nadia would be to the idea."

"I don't know how comfortable I am doing recon for your love life," Sydney hesitated.

"Come on, Syd! Help me out a little. Just ask a few discreet questions. Heck, look at it as an opportunity to keep your spying skills from getting rusty."

Sydney laughed a little at the ridiculousness of the request, but then she heard her call waiting beep again and realized it was probably Vaughn, thinking he'd been cut off and calling back. "Okay, okay. I'll see what I can do, but right now I have to go."

"You, Sydney, have incurred a debt from me. A life debt. No small thing, and something well worth having."

"Yeah, Eric. Look, I really have to—"

"Oh, of course! I should go too," Weiss said. "It's Showcase Showdown time!"

Wearily, Sydney hit the call waiting button again, and immediately launched into an apology. "I am so sorry," she effused, "but I just got the craziest call and couldn't get away."

She had, however, once again misjudged who was on the other line. "Sydney," came a woman's voice through a wall of sobs. "Sydney, I . . ." The voice dissolved into tears.

"Keiko?" Sydney sat bolt upright, all thoughts of Chinese food disappearing as she snapped into crisis mode. "Keiko, listen to me. Calm down. Tell me where you are, and I'll be right there."

Keiko had told Sydney that she was at a small public park in the Marina, close to the ocean. Sydney rushed there and wended her way through frolicking kids, Frisbee-catching dogs, and teenage girls lolling with their heads on their boyfriends' tanned stomachs, until she spied Keiko sitting morosely in the grass. She looked pretty, but very sad, and she seemed thin, perhaps even wasted away. Clad in a T-shirt and jeans, in contrast to her usual sharp dress, she flexed her toes absently in her flip-flops and stared glumly at her phone. Sydney guessed Keiko had hung up with her and then not moved since.

Sydney sat, dropping awkwardly down on her injured leg, and didn't say a word for several minutes. Keiko sniffled a few times, but otherwise she remained silent as well. The teary tension finally broke when Keiko's cell phone rang.

"It's Franklin," Keiko said, looking at the caller ID. She didn't move to answer it, and once it had rung three or four times, she stood and hurled it as far away from her as she could. Two kids watched, turning to each other questioningly when they saw it roll to a halt in the grass nearby. Keiko sat back down heavily, wiping her eyes with her fingers. The arm she'd fractured, freshly free of the cast she'd worn for the past month, looked emaciated and weak, and the rest of her seemed broken and unhealthy as well.

"Here, Keiko," Sydney said, holding out a small package of tissues. Keiko took them blankly, dabbing at her running makeup and blowing her nose noisily. Sydney looked away, giving her friend time to collect herself, but her eyebrows shot up when she stole a look at her friend's face. The pile of crumpled tissues growing next to Keiko was tinted with smeared-off cover-up, and Keiko's cheeks were purple with now visible bruises. A particularly nasty one puffed out around her right temple. Keiko registered Sydney's shock, and she offered a Sydney a fake smile of reassurance, betrayed by the tears that just kept coming.

"Look, K, I don't mean to press, but . . ." Sydney began.

"It's nothing!" Keiko snapped. "The bruises are from when I fell down and fractured that bone, and they still haven't quite healed." Sydney knew she was lying. An old hand at hiding bruises, she could tell at a glance that Keiko's were fresh.

Mustering a friendly shrug, Sydney offered a noncommittal "Okay." She bit her lip to make sure that the next word spoken would be said by Keiko. *If she really doesn't want to talk about this,* Sydney thought, *then I shouldn't force her to.*

It was a long silence. Running children made entire circuits around the park and countless Frisbees were tossed back and forth while Keiko visibly struggled with what she wanted to say. Sydney sat wrestling with her own impulse to speak, knowing that she would gladly take the burden of the conversation off her friend as soon as she could, but that for the moment it was best to simply wait and listen. They could hear Keiko's cell ring once again from its resting place in the grass.

Finally Keiko's head tipped downward, and she spoke quietly, as if addressing the grass beneath her and no one else. "Franklin sometimes gets a little rough."

Fury boiled in Sydney. She had spent days strapped in a dentist's chair while a sinister-looking Chinese man yanked on her molars with pliers, and still the desire to put the smackdown on Franklin Thornhill dwarfed any rage she had ever experienced. It took an incredible amount of willpower to restrain herself, but she knew that right now comforting Keiko, reassuring her that this wasn't her fault, and encouraging her to get help took priority.

"That's terrible," said Sydney, flinching at her own understatement. "And wrong. We'll make sure it never happens again."

"He does it because he loves me," Keiko insisted fiercely. "I know that women always say that, but this is different."

"People don't generally show their love with

their fists," Sydney countered gently. Though she wanted to correct Keiko's ridiculous sentiment more stridently, she knew that the last thing Keiko needed right now was to feel bullied in any way. "And whatever the reason behind what he's done, it doesn't matter. Because hurting you isn't right, and we can't let him do it anymore." She fished for something more to say, but it was hard. The obvious things seemed inappropriate, and the not-so-obvious ones seemed unimportant.

"This," Keiko began, gesturing vaguely toward the bruises on her face, "isn't even what really hurts me. I don't care. . . . I really don't. Lately I've been missing my dad a lot. And there's something else. . . ."

"What is it, K?"

Keiko was too overcome with sadness to go on. She submitted to Sydney's embrace as she bawled away, with Sydney speaking to her comfortingly and stroking her hair. A man jogging past with his collie gave them a sidelong glance, but Sydney's scowl sent him on his way. Keiko eventually looked up, cheeks wet and eyes red, when she heard the ring of her cell phone yet again. Sydney stood up, brushed herself off, and began to walk toward the phone.

"What are you doing?" Keiko asked.

"I'm going to tell him that you'll be staying with me while we get you help. I'm going to tell him not to be there when you come home to collect your things, and I'm going to tell him to stop calling."

"No, you can't!" Sydney stopped short, puzzled by the genuine terror in Keiko's voice. "He can't know I told you about this! I don't . . . I don't know what he'd do to you!"

Sydney didn't let herself smile, despite the fact that nothing would please her more than for Franklin to give her an excuse to let loose on him. *It's very sweet of you to worry about me, K,* she thought, *but I'm not quite the mild-mannered bank employee you think I am.* "I think I can handle myself," she finally said.

"No, Syd. No, no . . ." Keiko pulled Sydney back down to the grass, looking around fearfully. "Look, I know this is going to sound crazy, but, well . . . Listen . . ."

It all came out, in a wild torrent. Sydney tried her best to follow Keiko's story, but it wasn't easy. Strangely, much of it had nothing to do with Franklin. Keiko dug desperately through her purse until she found a tiny photo album and illustrated much of her explanation with pictures, pressing into Sydney's hands a sweet picture of her father, Hikaru Terajima, taken a long time ago, in better times. He appeared muscular and yet brainy in his thick glasses, which befitted his status as what Keiko called "a giant in the field of Japanese rocket science." She gazed at the picture and broke down yet again. "I haven't really spoken to him in years. He grew more and more distant after I married Franklin, and lately he doesn't even answer the phone when I call. We'd always been so close. We always went to baseball games together. We'd been best friends ever since my mother died. Here's a picture of her, you can see . . ."

"She's gorgeous," Sydney said. "She looks just like you."

"I always thought she had the prettiest name," Keiko said, fighting to produce a smile through her tears. "She left us when I was too young to really know her or have solid memories, but I always loved rolling her name around in my mouth. 'Midori.' It's just so pretty, like her. I could say it a thousand times and not get tired of it."

"It's lovely. But Keiko . . . none of this sounds too out of the ordinary."

Keiko went on to describe how Franklin had always seemed interested in her father's work, in a vaguely creepy sort of way, almost like he idolized the man. "I used to worry that he only married me to get close to my father," Keiko said jokingly, but the joke fell flat. "But then I realized he was just a strange man, my husband. He'd been so sweet when we were dating, and I fell so hard, Sydney."

Sydney tried to seem understanding, but looking at a picture of Franklin, she couldn't help thinking that even on film he was chilly. He'd seemed cold every time she'd met him over the last few weeks. Slickly European and off-puttingly formal, he had blond hair plastered back with copious amounts of gel, which in Sydney's mind was a deal breaker, and his speech had an odd lilt, like he'd learned to speak by listening to bad Cary Grant impressions. "Well, it's hard to see things clearly when you're first falling in love," Sydney offered.

"Here's the thing, though, Sydney." The sun was starting to set, and Keiko's skin glowed in the low light. The park was clearing out, and there was less noise to cover the things she was obviously uncomfortable saying, so she went on in a whisper. "Since we were first married, he's disappeared a few times. And there have been strange phone calls made to our house. Men have come to our door or been caught sneaking around our home, and they have not been nice men. Franklin's made them go away, but I think he might be . . ."

Sydney waited a moment, then prompted her to continue. "You think he might be what?"

"I know you won't believe me, Sydney. But I think he might be a spy."

CHAPTER 4

LOS ANGELES
LATER THAT DAY

It was just your basic office chair with a plush seat, adjustable back, and slightly worn armrests. One wheel squeaked a little. It was no more or less comfortable than any of the other chairs in the room. There was no reason for anyone not to have sat down in it when the meeting started. And yet it was left unoccupied.

The APO briefing room was like a high school English class, in that seats weren't assigned but there was an unspoken agreement that you didn't take someone else's spot. This particular chair was

Sydney's, which meant, since she was suspended, that it was empty. It also meant that Vaughn's eyes tended to fall on it whenever he glazed over during a briefing. Which happened often, especially lately.

He wasn't the only one having trouble focusing. More than once today, as Jack led the discussion, Vaughn had noticed that Nadia's eyes were drawn to Weiss's vacant seat, and on the occasions when their eyes met, she'd blushed a little in embarrassment at having been caught. Vaughn had also let his eyes stray a couple of times to a yellow pad that Marshall was using to take notes, and he'd watched as some idle scribbling had evolved into a complex sketch of clouds hanging heavily over a nighttime landscape. In a touch typical of Marshall, he'd labeled his doodles carefully: "Stratus," "Cumulonimbus," and so forth. He'd never pegged Marshall for an artist, but Vaughn couldn't help admiring the skill of his inkwork in the cirrus formations spilling out into the margins.

"As you all know, our preliminary reconnaissance in Malaysia hit an unexpected dead end," Jack was saying. "The unfortunate demise of Eddie Kim has left us with few leads to pursue in determining the reliability of numerous tips that the so-called Dark

Cloud terror cell is planning some kind of attack, nature undetermined, in the near future." They'd been over this again and again for weeks and had gotten nowhere. Vaughn was starting to think that Dark Cloud was a myth, a sort of Santa Claus for terrorists that was spoken of but was essentially a collective fantasy. He also wondered if the rumors of its nefarious plans were as empty as Sydney's chair.

"Dark Cloud is bent on undermining the balance of power in Asia," Nadia recounted. "But the nature of its connection to global terror networks and espionage organizations is unknown. Which means the attack is probably slated for somewhere in Asia, but even that isn't certain."

"There was that recent bit of chatter suggesting they're planning to use crop dusters in the strike," Dixon piped up. "It could be a 9/11-style hijack-and-crash scenario." This was a stab in the dark, and even Dixon himself didn't sound convinced.

"But crop dusters are designed to take off, make three passes over a field, and then land," Nadia mused skeptically.

"Right," agreed Marshall, "and zero range means they carry, like, almost no fuel. Crashing them into a building would cause a lot of noise, and obviously if you're in the building it might be pretty bad, but by terrorist standards, it'd be like attacking someone with a gnat. Like, 'Buzz-buzz-buzz! I'm buzzing around you, and maybe biting you a little! Aren't you eager to give up your imperialistic Western ways?' And the tall guy would be like, 'No! I like my Western ways just fine, thank you very much.' And he'd swat the gnat—"

"Your point is noted, Marshall," Jack said peremptorily, before clicking a button that made pictures of two men appear on the screen behind him. "It seems to me the focus of our investigation has to be on these men. The one on the left is Eddie Kim's half-Chinese half brother Fan Li, who is equally connected to the weapons trade, and equally difficult to locate." He gestured to Fan Li's glowering visage. He had scars all over his cheeks from countless street fights, but he still retained an odd sense of sophistication. "The second man—who to me is more alarming—is their Japanese associate and moneyman, Kiyoaki Honda." The man on the right wore thin-rimmed glasses and would have looked meek and mousy if he hadn't had a weird, leering expression on his face, like he was waiting for the camera shutter to sound so that he could lean in and lick the lens.

"Honda's linked to half a dozen bombings throughout Asia," Dixon said. "And yet he must have some well-connected friends, because he strolls the streets over there with complete impunity."

"I've known people who have been killed in his attacks," Jack said coldly. "Skilled agents, people with families. If I didn't think he could lead us to something significant in the Dark Cloud organization, I would say he has no business remaining alive."

The entire room fell silent at this vehement statement. This was a situation where the insight and good humor of their absent colleagues were much missed. Indeed, they felt all the absences: Sloane was abroad gathering intel, and Sydney and Weiss were still on recuperative leave, which meant the team could very much use some other perspectives. Even Jack seemed stymied.

Vaughn grew increasingly irritated by the silence. *This is going nowhere anyway,* he thought decisively.

"I'm going to get more coffee. It might help recharge my brain a little," he announced, standing and grabbing his coffee mug. It was Weiss's, and it featured a cartoon moose exclaiming, "Watch me pull a rabbit out of my hat!"

"You should have Baker do that," Nadia said weakly. Until a month ago, Weiss had been hazing the new junior agent rather mercilessly, shoveling reports, copy jobs, and cheeseburger-fetching tasks upon him with glee. Nadia had somewhat half-heartedly been attempting to keep the tradition alive in his absence.

Vaughn shrugged her suggestion aside and excused himself, leaving the stalled discussion behind and stepping out into the brightly lit APO corridor. The low hum of day-to-day espionage work filled the offices. Vaughn made his way down a hallway, passing by one of the more secluded research cubicles. The light was on. Curious to see if whoever was inside had any new info on Dark Cloud, he popped his head around the corner and found, to his delight, Sydney staring thoughtfully at a computer screen.

"Decided to shop for that Father's Day gift online, huh?" he asked. Sydney turned, startled, but lit up when she saw that it was Vaughn. "You're not supposed to be here, Syd, but I gotta say, I couldn't be more glad to see you."

"I'm glad to see you too," she said, but placed her hand on his chest to stop him from leaning in to kiss her. "Maybe you can figure out why the computer won't accept my password."

Vaughn seemed confused that she was being all businesslike but shrugged it off. "Well, you've been away for a month. Your clearances have to be brought up to date. What do you need? I can check it for you."

Sydney hesitated and tapped her cane nervously as she weighed just how much to share. It was an odd impulse she was feeling. Normally Vaughn would be the first person she went to in search of advice on a touchy matter, but now she felt herself holding back. Part of it was her near certainty that Keiko was overreacting, driven to a vulnerable place by abuse and growing paranoid about her abuser. Franklin was probably nothing more than a jerk who didn't know how to control his temper, and it was irresponsible to bring the massive hammer of APO resources down on a relatively simple domestic problem. But another part of it was a base desire, stemming from Vaughn's refusal to tell her about what was going on at APO these past few weeks, to have a secret of her own.

Vaughn claimed he was just yielding to Jack's orders to keep Sydney out of the loop, but then hadn't Keiko similarly asked Sydney to keep this to herself? *This is ridiculous,* Sydney finally forced herself to concede. *My friend needs help, and that's what's most important here. I can ask the man I love to help me help her.*

"I'm trying," she began slowly, "to find out a little about Keiko's husband, Franklin Thornhill."

"So you snuck in here to use the Interpol terminal?" Vaughn said skeptically. "Your basic Google search and credit check wouldn't do?"

"Keiko has some suspicions," Sydney offered, feeling a little silly as Vaughn tilted his head and gave her a what's-really-going-on-here look. "And he's not the best husband."

"You think that makes him a spy? Listen, Syd, just because you and I have known a few more Jacks and Sloanes than Marshalls and Dixons doesn't mean dysfunctional relationships are the hallmark of people who do spy work."

Sydney considered this, and she had to admit Vaughn was right. Still, she'd promised Keiko she'd look into it. "Will you please just poke around anyway? For me?"

Vaughn's smile changed, his quizzical look melting into one of mildly indulgent affection. Sydney smiled too. "I hear incurring a life debt is no small thing," she added flirtatiously.

"A life debt?"

"Something I heard someone say."

"Isn't that from *Star Wars*? One of the new ones, too, not the good ones?"

"Maybe the person I heard say it was lacking a little in the cool department."

Vaughn nodded, leaning down for that deferred kiss. Sydney let out her breath as she let him embrace her. Somehow, telling him about Keiko's problems had dispelled the momentary cloud between them, like a fan turned on after a kitchen mishap.

"I checked the systems, Miss Bristow," a youthful voice said, "and everything seems to be fine. Oh! I'm sorry, I didn't realize you were in a meeting." Sydney and Vaughn turned around quickly to find Mark, the new junior agent, standing in the doorway. "I, uh . . . I just . . . I think it's just that your password is out of date."

"Yeah, I figured that out, Mark. Thanks for looking into it, though," Sydney said.

Mark turned and left.

"I should probably go before I get in trouble with my dad," Sydney said, turning to face Vaughn. "Will you let me know what you find out on Franklin?"

"I'll tell you over dinner. And we won't invite Mark, okay?" Vaughn watched Sydney shake her head, willing some nagging thoughts away. "What? Something's bothering you, Syd."

"I just . . . I feel bad for Keiko. All she's ever wanted was a first edition of *Light in August* and a ring on her finger, and the person she thought she was building a life with isn't who she thought he was."

Now it was Vaughn's turn to grow a little distant. Something was troubling him, and Sydney caught it immediately.

"Are you keeping something from me, Vaughn?" she asked playfully, but he remained a little dark.

"It seems to me—" Vaughn stopped himself, then started over. "I think a relationship where you know everything there is to know about the other person is a relationship that has no room to grow." It seemed like he was about to tell her something important, but he settled for: "I hope we never stop surprising each other, Syd."

Sydney considered this and decided to keep the mood light. "I wouldn't mind," she said, "if your next surprise glittered and hung around my neck."

They laughed and kissed good-bye, and Sydney made her way back out on her cane, leaving Vaughn sitting thoughtfully by the computer terminal. With a shrug, he logged into the computer system and typed Franklin Thornhill's name in at the prompt. *Might as well get this done so I can get back to banging my head against the wall over crop dusters,* he thought.

It took a moment for the computer to process Franklin's name. Vaughn drummed his fingers on the table while he waited, expecting to receive a terse record of mundane passport checks, maybe a drunk-and-disorderly citation from a wild night decades before. Instead, the computer spat out page after page of information.

Vaughn began scanning the readout. With each page his eyes grew wider.

CHAPTER 5

BERLIN
THAT NIGHT

The kid looked like he was about to cry.

Most young people his age would kill to be in his position, to suddenly find themselves on a brightly lit stage before a crowd of adoring female fans. The fans' boyfriends, any of whom would have had to go home alone if the kid were to desire a companion for the evening, stood aloof toward the back of the small club, sipping sodas and envying him. Booked into tiny venues by a record company that had seriously underestimated American emo music's appeal in Europe, the young man was greeted at each train station and airport by mobs, and tickets to this show were going for an astronomical amount of money on the street outside. You'd think he'd be feeling on top of the world. But he looked profoundly sad, on the verge of tears, like he was sure he was doomed to die alone.

Brushing his shaggy hair out of his eyes and giving the room a simperingly dewy look, he went back to strumming his guitar as he led his solo acoustic number into its overwrought climax, crooning its angst-ridden lyrics in a voice full of tremulous whine.

I will stay with you come what may
Listening to the raindrops hit the pane
Through the thunderstorms and hurricanes
Waiting for the beauty after rain . . .

The kid finished his song and took a modest, pained bow as the audience exploded in wild applause. Standing at the back of the room, lounging at the bar and running his finger idly around the rim of an untouched drink, Arvin Sloane rolled his eyes, unimpressed. Admittedly, the music wasn't exactly targeted at him: He was approximately three times the age of the average member of the singer's fan base, and the whole musical package seemed specifically designed for the other end of the emotional spectrum from the cold, unfeeling world that was Sloane's home turf. Sloane himself had often felt it might kill him if he were to betray an emotion, and like the singer, a smile would seem completely unnatural on his face. But then Sloane was no longer a young man, and the knowledge that the unguarded expression of emotion was a weakness was exactly the kind of wisdom this kid's music so sorely lacked.

Not that Sloane was paying the music much attention. Instead, he was scanning the crowd for an old contact, Ferdinand Crosby, a low-level mover and shaker in the chemical weapons trade who had known Sloane since this kid's parents were kids themselves. He hadn't seen Crosby in years, and a lack of upward mobility in his chosen profession notwithstanding, Crosby had always been quite skilled at disguise, which meant that Sloane wasn't even sure he'd recognize the man he was to meet. Still, he was pretty sure Crosby would stand out in the crowd. Why his contact had suggested this club for a rendezvous was beyond Sloane, who couldn't think of a place where two old men would look more conspicuous.

He'd inspected everyone in the room over twenty years old, determining that they were either bouncers or bootleggers or creepy types who liked leering at underage girls. The whisper-quiet and stock-still crowd afforded no room for Ferdinand to hide, and Sloane felt reasonably certain that so long as he kept an eye on the entrances—one from the street and two from a stockroom and a backstage area behind the club—he could mark Crosby's appearance and prevent him from gaining the upper hand through surprise. Crosby was an old friend, but that would mean little if any of Sloane's numerous rivals were to make the slightest effort to convince Crosby that switching friendships was to his advantage.

Sloane clenched his teeth, expecting the worst, when he felt a tap on his shoulder and heard a soft "Good evening" whispered from behind him. When a moment passed without Sloane feeling the butt of a gun or the blade of a knife in his back, he let his muscles relax as he turned to see what disguise the chameleon had adopted today. What he saw caused one of his eyebrows to rise, an expression of considerable shock by Sloane's standards.

"You're looking well," said the heavily pierced and obscenely tattooed teenager in a low voice. "Though you're dressed a little conservatively for this crowd, I must say."

Sloane leaned in to speak directly into the boy's ear. "You have the wrong man."

"You don't recognize your old pal Ferdinand?" the teenager chortled, receiving an annoyed shush from a trendy showgoer standing nearby. Nodding apologetically, the boy lowered his tone and added, "Or are you just feeling out of place, Arvin, and wishing you had my powers of camouflage?" He reached out for Sloane's drink, but Sloane grabbed his wrist and the boy froze.

"No disguise can take forty years off a man's age. Who are you?"

"If I were anyone but Ferdinand Crosby," the teenager responded brightly, "how could I remember so accurately every second of an evening in Havana twenty-five years ago?"

"Was that you?" Sloane answered. "All I really remember from that night is the blond casino girl Ferdinand and I sent up to Castro's room to distract him."

"Funny, I could have sworn there were two casino girls. And they were redheads." Sloane nodded, puzzled, as the boy passed the little test. "And if they were meant merely as a distraction, why did we give them both loaded pistols to tuck in their garters?"

"Okay, okay," muttered Sloane.

"But I don't blame you for trying to forget that night. You were pretty sweet on one of the girls, weren't you? The closest thing to sadness I ever saw on your face was when her body landed right at our feet after Castro's guards threw her off that balcony."

"Will you please to be quiet?" came a sharp rebuke from nearby.

Crosby snarled back rudely in fluent German. "Shut up, trash. I'm having a conversation with this geezer here, so shove it."

This Ferdinand was more like the one Sloane knew and tolerated. But the mode of expression rang wrong. No matter how skilled his physical impression might be, Ferdinand could never have replicated the slang-ridden German speech of a Berlin teen. Feigning a letting down of his guard, Sloane offered an approximation of a smile. They say it takes more muscles to frown than to smile, but for Sloane, perhaps because the muscles were used so little, the smiling muscles always seemed stiff. He turned to the bar and ordered a drink for "Ferdinand," as well as one for the annoyed guy nearby, who accepted it and nodded, mollified.

As "Ferdinand" turned to knock back the drink,

Sloane saw a wire snaking up the back of his neck, almost invisible as it threaded through an intricate and rather unsettling tattoo of what looked like a 1950s-era American housewife eating a goat. Once he knew what he was looking for, it wasn't hard to see how it wended through a large metal ring embedded in the boy's earlobe and disappeared into his ear canal.

The singer onstage was building to another of his sodden crescendos, imploring an unseen girlfriend to do something or other, when Sloane set down his drink, and with as much visible exertion as most people give to fumbling sleepily for the television remote, hooked his arm around the teenager's ink-stained skull and pounded his face down onto the bar, smashing his nose. Blood began to flow through the pools of condensation on the bartop. The music stopped abruptly.

"What's going on out there?" the kid asked from the stage as the entire crowd turned to look at Sloane. Sloane paid them no mind as he pulled the wire out, producing a spurt of blood as he tugged the metal loop free from the boy's earlobe. A tiny earpiece was at the end of the wire, and after sanitizing it in a nearby glass of vodka, Sloane tucked it in his own ear.

"What's going on, Gustav?" he heard, Crosby's real voice recognizable through the tiny speaker.

"Where's Ferdinand?" Sloane hissed menacingly in the boy's bloody ear. "Inside the club, or out?"

"This is not a place for fighting," the singer insisted earnestly. "Let's just cool it and listen to some music, okay?" His tears seemed even more likely to flow now. Sloane ignored all of this.

"In or out?" he growled.

"In the club," grunted the boy finally, spitting blood onto the bar when Sloane released him. "I don't know where."

It was at just this moment that a bartender poked her head out from the storeroom, and Sloane glanced in to see that it was otherwise empty. Striding through the fascinated crowd as if they weren't even there, he moved toward the door to backstage, and as he disappeared through it, he could hear the kid leaning into his microphone and intoning his verdict on what had just happened. "Old people," he said ominously. "Don't turn into one."

The music resumed. Backstage, Sloane purposefully opened door after door until he found

Crosby, looking old and dressed quite plainly, sitting in a cramped, brightly lit dressing room, turning dials on a tiny transmitter. "Gustav?" he was barking into a tiny mike. "Gustav, are you there?" He trailed off as he noticed Sloane. After a long, awkward moment, he raised his hand weakly and waved.

Sloane tossed the tiny earpiece at Crosby's feet. The metal ring that had previously been lodged in the boy's earlobe made a hollow noise as it hit the floor.

"I've never understood the appeal of piercings," Sloane said coolly.

"How are you, Arvin?"

"The intelligent man, after all, will do just about anything to keep his skin intact. Faced with the prospect of having metal pierce it, he will fight, or flee, or forget all principle and cooperate even with his deadliest enemy."

"I apologize," stammered Crosby. "It was rude not to meet you face-to-face."

"And yet, young people today take pleasure in doing to themselves what I, and many in my profession, have done forcibly to those we despise in order to torture them into submission. This is odd, don't you think?"

"Uh, yes." Crosby thought for a moment, then decided he had nothing more to say. "Yes."

"Gustav, I suspect, will be less enthusiastic about future piercings, and for that I honestly think he owes me a heartfelt thanks."

"He was a front, obviously," Crosby said. "I wasn't sure I could trust you."

"I'd suggest he buy me a drink to show his appreciation, but I doubt he's old enough."

Crosby fell silent. Sloane nodded, then pulled up a chair. The room was so small that Sloane's knees knocked into Crosby's as he sat. Crosby sat up straight and offered an explanation for his actions.

"I've heard, Arvin, that your loyalties have gotten even slipperier since we last met. I felt it would be best to keep some distance between us, but that plan—"

"I'm told you have information on the Dark Cloud sect," Sloane said flatly.

Crosby stammered a moment, then switched gears. "See I know this guy," Crosby mused, "who knows a guy who's been hearing things about crop dusters."

Sloane was silent. Crosby seemed to need

prompting, but Sloane felt that inflicting pain still seemed a tad premature. "Yes, we've heard something about that ourselves," he said blandly.

"Well, I got interested," Crosby said, leaning forward, warming to his topic. "Just from a professional standpoint. It seemed a little old-fashioned, when almost all the major developments in chemical weapons the last couple of decades have focused on increasingly sophisticated delivery systems. Using crop dusters would be like arming special ops soldiers with bows and arrows. So I started poking around. And these Dark Cloud guys, they're smart guys. The best of the bunch were the Kim brothers."

"Eddie and Fan Li Kim, you mean."

"Exactly."

Sloane nodded, the fact that his patience was wearing thin remaining completely disguised. "Which leads us where, Ferdinand?"

"Which leads us," Crosby said, wiggling his fingers, "to this." He reached into his jacket pocket, pulling out a tiny vial of liquid. Sloane took it and sloshed the liquid around curiously.

"I stole it from Fan Li the last time we met. He seemed disappointed that I had, uh, misrepresented the quality of some materials I was trying to sell him, which I think was more of a misunderstanding. I didn't realize he wanted enough rifles for an army's worth of guards. Anyway, I palmed this before he stormed out of the meeting."

"What is it?"

"I don't know. But I think you oughta be making a ton of it."

Crosby blinked brightly, certain that he had just made Sloane's day. Sloane pursed his lips, nodded twice, then reached around and placed a hand on Crosby's shoulder affectionately. Crosby withered immediately, but he couldn't slump down in his seat. Sloane had him pinned in place, obviously in a great deal of pain. For his part, Sloane seemed to be doing nothing more than clapping an arm around a good friend.

"I can't help noticing, Ferdinand," he said matter-of-factly, "that the address on the side of this vial is from a Japanese conglomerate located in suburban Osaka. Yet you say you stole it from a Chinese diplomat with a Korean last name. You'll forgive me if I find it hard to believe you're being straightforward."

Sweat beaded on Crosby's forehead, shining brightly in the dressing-room light as if he was wearing a crystal-studded tiara. "You've known me a long time, Arvin. I've never been anything more than a dot." He grunted, clearly losing his struggle to keep from crying out in pain. "And we dots don't know anything about what the lines connecting us draw."

Convinced, Sloane released him and stood up, his attention laser-focused on the vial.

"Two pieces of advice, Arvin," Crosby said, rubbing his neck tenderly. Sloane looked at him placidly. "One, if you really want to know what that stuff is, you have to ask Fan Li Kim. And two, you need to start saying thank you with words, not gestures."

Sloane tucked the vial away in his breast pocket. As he exited the room, he turned and said, "Two for you in return, my friend. One, never mention a dead young girl to a living old man. And two, you really ought to start listening to better music."

CHAPTER 6

LOS ANGELES
SEVERAL DAYS LATER

She could replay it in her mind effortlessly.

The ornate jar filled with pencils and pens, nudged closer to the edge of the desk by the papers she was shuffling through, tipped over and fell, remaining visible through the glass desktop until it hit the floor. It spent maybe half a second in midair, the writing implements clustered together in the jar the entire way down before they spilled over the rug, scattering everywhere. That half second flashed before her like an amateur video run and rerun on the evening news, and she could stop it, back it up, even zoom in. She did so again and again as she knelt, gathering up the pens frantically and trying to replace them in the jar exactly as they had been before the spill. *Does Franklin put his pencils away point down or eraser down?* she wondered, trying to remain calm. Repeated mental replays had her almost, but not quite, convinced that the writing ends of the pens were all invisible before the jar tumbled, so she put them back point first. But she wasn't entirely sure. She tried turning them all over, but that looked wrong too. And then when she rose to put the jar back on the desk, she saw that her knees had made two faint circular recesses in the rug. *Stop being paranoid, Keiko,* she scolded herself. *They're barely noticeable.* She rubbed them away with her toe nevertheless.

Her husband would be home any minute. He'd just gone to run his usual Sunday errands, and they never took long. It embarrassed her that she'd wasted quite a bit of what little time she had in trying to decide whether or not to don gloves for her projected five-minute rummage through her husband's office. She had skipped the gloves. Now, irrationally certain that incriminating fingerprints were visible on every surface in the room, she found herself regretting it.

But there was no time to think about that. She'd barely begun her search, and already the five minutes she'd given herself had stretched into ten. Admittedly, she'd found plenty of eyebrow-raising stuff already: a long list of telephone numbers she recognized as Japanese, Chinese, and Korean, as well as a set of articles about her father photocopied from foreign magazines. Certain passages from the interviews—complex ruminations on telemetry and payload capability—were highlighted in pink or yellow, and Franklin had made extensive, almost illegible notations in the margins. None of this proved that anything sinister was going on, necessarily, but her curiosity was piqued. She had to continue the search, despite the fact that it was probably a very bad idea to have started it in the first place.

In fact, Sydney had come out and told her it was a very bad idea, and generally speaking, she knew she should listen to Sydney. But the other girl—Nadia, was it?—had made a fine, giggling case for its being only kind of a bad idea, rather than very bad, and somehow the idea had nagged at Keiko all night until, when morning came, she rose from bed resolved to go ahead and do it. *The dangers of hatching plans while drinking,* Keiko thought to herself grimly. *Or maybe it would be more apt to say the dangers of hatching plans while bowling. . . .*

A Saturday "Girls' Night Out" had sounded great, and Keiko had accepted the invitation gratefully, glad to get her mind off her troubles at home. Sydney had also asked this girl named Nadia to join them. Keiko hadn't quite followed who Nadia was—she thought she heard Sydney say she was her sister, but how could Sydney have a sister who was, like, Spanish or something? That didn't make much sense. She must have misheard. Anyway, it seemed Nadia had been on an intense bowling kick lately, because she was seeing some guy, a coworker who got her into it, and so the three girls had gone to a bowling alley in Santa Monica. It had been fun, Keiko thought, despite the fact that Sydney was still hobbling around and therefore couldn't participate, while Keiko had proved to be one of the least naturally gifted bowlers the sport had ever seen. After one of her stray gutter balls had actually leaped over into the next lane, incensing three potbellied guys who obviously took their bowling very, very seriously, Keiko had been amused that Sydney and Nadia were so unruffled by the bowlers' boozy threats, because the guys looked like they could have snapped either of the girls in two. And then Nadia had suggested that they adjourn to the adjoining bar for a few drinks.

Nadia proved to be a lot of fun, though she was almost as circumspect about her job as Sydney. *Whatever,* Keiko had thought as she'd ordered another round, *I guess some people don't like to talk about work during their nights off.* But in contrast to Sydney's quiet good-naturedness, and worlds away from Keiko's preoccupied gloom, Nadia was all laughs, and though none of them got drunk, a little tipsiness only added to the gaiety. Before long, Nadia was appreciatively nudging Keiko and Sydney into story after story about old times.

"So let me get this straight," Nadia said, laughing, at one point. "The girl had a tattoo of a skull-and-crossbones on her upper arm?"

"She had tons of tattoos. It was legendary around school," Sydney explained. "Every time she raised her hand—and keep in mind that she raised it constantly—her sleeve kind of fell down a little, and you could see that above the skull tattooed on her wrist, there was a little scroll that read 'Abandon hope.'"

Keiko was unsteadily spinning her empty glass on the wet countertop. "And the rumor around the department was that her other arm had a matching skull that said, 'All ye who,'" she said darkly, "which meant that you couldn't help wondering where the last two words in the phrase were tattooed."

Nadia giggled, covering her mouth modestly. "That's terrible," she said, obviously not at all troubled by the terribleness.

"She was a total brownnoser, that girl. She deserved the reputation."

"Keiko!" Sydney scolded.

"Well, she did!" Keiko responded indignantly.

Nadia slurred just a little as she put in her two cents. "That reminds me of the sort of thing you see in Japan," she said. "People involved in organized crime, especially, take their tattoos really seriously, and these complicated stories are inked all over them sometimes. I saw this one guy once who had an entire kabuki play running down one arm, across his chest, and then on until you got to the very bloody finale on his opposite hand. Amazing stuff."

"How on earth have you seen a yakuza tattoo?" Keiko laughed incredulously.

"I travel to Japan sometimes, and—" Nadia began, before Sydney cut her off.

"Nadia watches the Learning Channel a lot," Sydney interrupted. The two girls exchanged odd looks, which left Keiko a little puzzled.

"But," Keiko put in after an awkward moment, "you say you travel there? Because I grew up in Japan. Do you go for work, or . . ."

Nadia had yielded, apparently, to whatever little look Sydney had given her, and she waved the subject aside. "I just . . . I go now and then. The usual business trip kind of thing. So, Sydney says you still have family in Tokyo?"

Out in the lanes the loud crack of a strike was followed by a round of cheers. Somehow the sound spilling into the bar broke the tension, and Keiko smiled and reached into her purse to dig out one of her father's business cards. She also located a pen and scrawled a number on the back before handing it to Nadia. "This is my father's private cell. You should ring him up next time you're in Tokyo. If you can get him to answer—and I've had some trouble lately myself—he's an excellent guide to all the back-alley spots that tourists never stumble across. Unless you're, I don't know, fluent in Japanese and a master of disguise or something, you'd never even know his kind of hangouts exist."

Nadia—was she hiding a hint of a smile?—accepted the card gratefully and tucked it in her pocket. She seemed genuinely touched that Keiko would make the gesture, and the next round of drinks tasted wonderful. By the time the liquid in the girls' glasses was drained, they were laughing loudly and joking like the best of friends.

"So you've got to tell me how things are going with Eric," Sydney prodded Nadia clumsily. "Any plans to take things to the next level?" Keiko hid her face in her hands in sympathetic shame. She'd been out of the matchmaking business for a while now, but as rusty as she was, she knew this was no way to go about it. She decided to throw her old friend a bone.

"Sydney! Why would you even wonder about that? A gorgeous, smart girl like this, her love life is going exactly as well as she wants it to. I'm sure this Eric, whoever he is, is eating out of her hand."

"I'm sure," stammered Sydney. "I was just . . ."

"You were just asking questions when instead you should be offering advice." Keiko felt an old, long-dormant thrill stirring in her, and she started into a little speech with considerable gusto. "You see, Nadia, there are women out there who enjoy relationships because they offer a chance to be controlled, but a strong woman like you should be the one controlling them. If this guy—what's his name? Eric?"

"Yes." Nadia nodded, grinning. "He's the one who got me into bowling."

Keiko crinkled her nose. "Oh. Well. No matter. . . ." She imagined this beautiful woman spending her Friday nights rolling heavy balls down these filthy alleys with some overweight lunkhead like the guys in the next lane, and she felt a little sad. *A girl like this deserves a more exciting life than that!* she thought. *In fact, every girl deserves better than to be a mere prop in a man's life. . . .* A lump crept into Keiko's throat, but she banished it and plunged ahead. "Well, the point is, a strong woman like you should be in charge of the relationship. She should never let her man raise his hand. . . ."

"Raise his hand? Like the tattooed girl in your lectures?" Nadia giggled, but Sydney looked concerned, patting Keiko gently on the shoulder.

"She meant, 'have the upper hand,'" offered Sydney, but the conversation ended there, as Keiko dissolved into tears. Nadia's cheerful expression faded instantly, and the next few minutes were lost in Sydney's concern, Nadia's confusion, and Keiko's sobbing.

"I'm so sorry," she finally croaked. "Sometimes it just hits me, unexpectedly." She blew her nose, then composed herself. "I'm okay," she said with finality. "I've been having some trouble at home, Nadia."

"You don't need to talk about it, K," Sydney said quickly, but Nadia apparently didn't feel like letting it drop.

"No, what's the deal, Keiko?" she asked. "Fight with your husband or what?" Sydney tried to gently reprove Nadia, but whereas Keiko had grown teary with drink, Nadia seemed emboldened and shot through with a no-nonsense attitude. "Look, I know we don't know each other very well, but it seems to me that married women usually at least mention their husbands over the course of two hours of conversation. They can't help it. But you haven't even told me his name. Clearly there's something going on." She sat back, folding her arms across her chest, apparently set on waiting until Keiko fessed up.

Keiko exchanged a few blank blinks with Sydney, but she felt that the cloud had been dispelled. It wasn't due so much to the lack of sympathy she was getting from Nadia, as it was Nadia's refusal to coddle her, and this made her problems seem like ones she could deal with if only she'd articulate them and decide how best to approach them. "Well," she started, finding her footing surprisingly solid, "I think my husband may be up to no good."

"What kind of 'no good'?" asked Nadia, leaning forward. "And what can we do to stop him?"

Keiko explained her suspicions to Nadia, in clearer tones than she'd been able to offer Sydney. Nadia nodded avidly, listening and asking occasional perceptive questions, before giving her opinion on a course of action.

"If you ask me," she said, "you need to poke through his things a bit, gather some information."

"You mean, spy on him?"

"No, she doesn't mean that," Sydney said hastily.

"Actually, that's exactly what I mean, Syd. If I'm understanding you right, Keiko, you don't really know much about your husband. Don't feel bad about that," she added quickly, noticing a pained look on Keiko's face. "There are secrets in almost every relationship." Keiko swore she noticed Sydney biting her lip at this. "But if you really want to know why he's so interested in your father, and if you really don't feel you can come out and ask him about it, I think you need to do a little reconnaissance. Does he have a study or an office, someplace he works in private?"

"Yes. He has an office."

"Well, then, find a time when he's going to be out for an hour, go in there, and look through his stuff."

"Okay," announced Sydney. "Nadia's officially done drinking for the night. You don't know what you're talking about, Sis."

"Of course I do. Start with his desk. Go through the trash, which usually yields nothing, but it's worth a try. Then look at everything on the desktop, page through it. The real interesting stuff will be in the drawers, of course, but you need to get the lay of the land first. Maybe check the bookcases, too, in case there's something tucked behind a particular volume. Though that can take a little too much time, I guess, if you're not careful."

"Wow, you sound like you really know what you're talking about," marveled Keiko.

"She doesn't," Sydney insisted. "It's a very bad idea."

"Come on, Syd. This is an in-and-out kind of thing. Ten minutes and she'll know for sure what's going on. You could do the snooping for her. . . . You'd probably be better at it than she would."

"I'd be better at it than you, too. 'Go through the trash.' You've been reading a lot of John LeCarre novels lately, have you?"

"I said the drawers would be the key. I was just getting her warmed up."

Keiko's eyes moved brightly from Nadia to Sydney and back again. "Working at a bank, you develop some unusual skills, huh?"

Both Sydney and Nadia had laughed, and Sydney had skillfully steered the conversation away from Nadia's rifling-through-Franklin's-office idea. The rest of the evening had been spent in more idle conversation, and Sydney and Nadia had probably forgotten this little blip in the evening.

But Keiko hadn't. Which is why, having gotten the lay of the land, she was now moving on to the drawers.

Central drawer: tape, stapler, a bunch of rubber bands, and more pens. What was the deal with Franklin and writing implements? First drawer, left-hand side: a stack of printouts covered in chemical formulas. Nothing unusual for a lab technician. Bottom drawer, left-hand side: miscellaneous computer equipment, some old credit card receipts, and a stack of ticket stubs from every movie Franklin and Keiko had ever seen together. *Aw, that's sweet!* Keiko found herself thinking wistfully. But she quickly shook the sentiment aside and moved on. First drawer, right-hand side: a pile of clippings from an opera magazine. *Franklin sure does love opera,* she thought, riffling through the pile and finding nothing out of the ordinary. Finally she went to open the last drawer, the bottom one on the right-hand side.

It seemed to be locked.

Locked?

Keiko pulled at it, and found it wouldn't open. That was strange. She rattled it, hoping it might just be stuck, but it wouldn't budge. However, she did notice a tiny corner of a loose piece of paper slipping through the space between the drawer and the body of the desk. Unable to resist, she yanked on the paper, and it came free from inside the drawer. She looked at it carefully, and her mouth dropped open.

It was a transcript, in blocky Courier font and time-stamped, of a phone conversation she had had with her dad a few weeks earlier. Her dad had been standoffish as always, and she had tried to pry a little personal information out of him. But he had said almost nothing. The conversation was utterly forgettable, and if Keiko weren't so starved for conversations with her father she would have forgotten it herself, but she remembered every word, and apparently Franklin did as well. After all, he had taken the trouble to record it and type it out, every "um" and "er." If there was something sinister she'd been hoping to find, she'd found it.

And that was when Keiko heard the telltale sound of the front door opening.

"Keiko, my love? Are you here, hon?"

Franklin sounded relaxed and cheerful. Keiko, however, felt trapped and desperate. She tried to shove the transcript back through the thin space into the drawer, but she couldn't fit it back in, at least not at her current level of panic, and she rattled the drawer in an effort to pry the space a little wider.

"Where are you, darling? I brought you something!"

Giving the drawer one last desperate pull, Keiko found, to her horror, that the lock broke free and the drawer came open, a chunk of the lock still stuck to the drawer's lip. Inside was a stack of strange surveillance photos of an older man she didn't recognize.

She had no idea what to do. She'd never done anything like this before, and neither Nadia nor Sydney had offered any solid advice on how to proceed if something like this happened.

She heard Franklin's footsteps as he walked down the hall toward his office, and she grew tense with fear. What would he do when he found her in here? How could she possibly explain? She felt herself fading away, a familiar feeling that always came over her when she felt threatened by him.

Think, Keiko! You've got to do something! But what?

CHAPTER 7

LOS ANGELES
THAT VERY INSTANT

Note to self: Do not leave your cell phone on the bedside table at night. Leave it outside of arm's reach, so you'll have a good excuse for not answering when it rings at, like, eight in the morning on a Sunday. Oh, wait! The fact that it's eight in the morning on a Sunday is already a good excuse for not answering! So roll over and go back to sleep. If it's important, they'll call back.

They're calling back. Huh. Didn't expect that to happen quite so soon. Why don't they have "do not disturb" signs for phones? Whoever's on the other end of the line, didn't you get the message? I'm sleeping, and I'm not going to pick up. So cool it for now, and call back at a decent hour, all right? Okay, back to beddy-bye . . .

What? Again? Really? Okay, time to face facts: They're not going to stop calling until I answer. All right, then. Gotta sit up.

Whoa! Who left the room set on "spin"? Supplementary note to self: Do not drink even relatively small amounts of bowling-alley liquor. That stuff really packs a punch the next morning. Okay, pull it together. Ignore the queasiness and the general sense that waking you up at this hour is a borderline unforgivable offence. Reach out, find the phone, and try to sound pleasant when answering.

"Hello?"

Pretty good. I almost sounded conscious.

"Sydney! Help me! I'm here, and I broke the drawer, and Franklin just came home, and there's, like, transcripts and pictures, and he's down the hall, but he'll walk in here any minute, and I don't know what to do!"

"Keiko? Do you know what time it is?" *It's funny, but I was just dreaming of Keiko, wasn't I? She was rolling a gutter ball that bounced over into another lane. That was a dream, wasn't it? A bowling ball can't do that in real life, can it? Gosh, it's really too early to be thinking about this stuff. . . .*

"Sydney! I'm serious! I did what you and Nadia suggested, and I snuck into Franklin's office. And I broke the lock on one of his desk drawers, and I spilled his pens, but I think I took care of that, and he's home! Do you understand, Sydney? He's home! Which means he's going to come in here, where I am!"

Oh, my god. She didn't. She wouldn't have, right? "Keiko, we were joking around about doing that. Nadia was just . . ."

"That's a sailed ship, Sydney! I'm stuck in here. And I don't know what the deal is with you and your sister, or whoever that is, but you guys seem to know a thing or two about being sneaky. I didn't know who else to call."

"Okay. Gosh, Keiko . . ." *Snap out of it. Focus: Solve the problem. What are we looking at here? She's in a room, one exit probably, husband outside. He may or may not be an enemy agent, but he has a history of violence against her. I have to remove him from proximity to Keiko, then get her to safety. What are my options? Let's see. . . . I have to remember the layout of their house from that time she showed me around: His office was—where? End of the far hallway, opposite from the kitchen and the bedroom. I guess I could . . . oh, man, this is a seriously half-baked plan, but . . .*

"K, are you calling from your cell?"

"Yes. I didn't want him to see the extension-in-use light. Why?"

"Hang on."

Up, up, up. Get up. Just toss the bedspread on the floor. Never mind that it's been ages since I last vacuumed. Oh, man—I wish I was a little less groggy, thinking clearer, steadier on my feet. But no time to think about that: Gotta find the landline. Where is that stupid cordless? On the coffee table? No: just a bunch of hockey magazines and last night's dishes. Not on the couch, not by the armchair. Must be in the kitchen . . .

"Sydney, um . . ."

"Working on it, K. Sit tight."

"His footsteps are getting closer!"

There it is! Why doesn't Michael put it back in the cradle where it belongs? I really should talk to him about that later on. Now, though, I just have to think fast: Dial, and quickly!

"What's your landline again, K? 555-67 something?"

"678 . . ."

"6785, right. Got it. Hold on, and stay quiet."

It's ringing. It sounds funny, with a phone at each ear. It's loud through the landline in my left ear, and if I listen closely, I can hear it in my right ear through the cell, ringing in Keiko's house. Weird. Anyway: Come on, Franklin. Pick up. Sure, the temptation at this time on a Sunday is to let it go to voice mail, but pick it up anyway. You know you want to. What if it's something important, right? What if it's one of your spy buddies, or a pal from Wifeslappers Anonymous? No, calm down. Stay centered. I have to talk civilly to the guy in a minute here. . . .

"He's turning around, Sydney! He's going back to answer the phone in the living room!"

"Good, K. Be ready to make a break out of the office while I distract him."

"Syd, if he's in the living room, I can't get out without passing by him. He'll know I was in here!"

Deep breath. This is a fixable problem. Think it through.

"Good morning, Thornhill residence." *The guy always sounds so pleasant, if a little chilly. Not really friendly. All surface, giving nothing away from underneath. Like a spy, come to think of it.*

"Hi, um . . . is this Franklin? It's Sydney."

"Sydney!" *Nice of him to at least pretend to be delighted, despite the hour. If he wasn't hurting my friend in a completely unforgivable way, I might even reach a point where I could tolerate him.* "What brings you to our phone so early, my dear?"

"You've got to get him to move farther into the house, Sydney! So I can sneak out!" *Hold your horses, K! I'm working on it.*

"Well, Franklin, I, uh . . ." *What am I supposed to say? Where's that much-vaunted thinking-on-my-feet mental spryness that makes me the toast of APO? Oh, right. I left it back in my bedroom, sleeping off a mild hangover. Come up with something, take the plunge:* "I'm supposed to meet Keiko for breakfast." *Sounds believable. Keep going. Add some detail, but not too much. A lie is always better as a sketch than a painting.* "Yesterday was so fun we didn't want the night to end. But it was late, so we came up with this breakfast plan. I don't think we realized how early the morning would feel when it arrived." *Why don't I force a little chuckle while I'm at it, really sell it. Nice: He's chuckling too. I've got him hooked.*

"Oh, well, that explains it! I wondered where she was when I came home just now. But if you're calling to tell her you'll be late, you'd do better to try her mobile. She seems to have already left."

Okay, now reel him in: "Oh, no. That's not why. I was actually calling because . . . well, this is embarrassing, but I can't remember where we were supposed to meet. And I'd rather not admit to her that I've forgotten. Makes me look like the airhead I am, you know." *Yuck. That was too much. 'Sydney Bristow, mild-mannered former grad student' is the hardest alias I've ever had. . . .*

"I understand. Well, I do wish I could help, but she didn't mention the appointment to me. She's always a bit mysterious, that one. Never know what she's up to." *What's that you're calling the kettle, Mr. Pot? Ugh. But I've got to keep the disgust out of my voice. Keep it light.*

"Well, I was hoping maybe she wrote it down in her, um . . . in her appointment calendar."

"What appointment calendar?"

"Yeah, Syd. What appointment calendar? What are you talking about?" *Hush up, Keiko! I'm working here.*

"You know, Franklin! In the appointment calendar she keeps by her bed. Always checks it every night before she goes to sleep, so she knows what's coming up the next day? She used to say in grad school that it was the only thing that kept her organized." *This isn't going well. He's never going to fall for it. Sunday morning subterfuge is not my specialty. But now that I'm digging the hole, I'd better keep digging.* "It would really help me out if you'd look."

"Honey, my wife was a literature grad student. I don't think organization was even something she aspired to."

"Could you just check? Right by her bed? Um, your bed, I guess."

"Well, I'll see. But I've been married to Keiko for a while now. I think I'd have noticed." *He's grumbling a little, sounding put out. Doesn't really matter, pal, so long as you move back into the bedroom and away from the office.* "Let's see here. I'm heading for the bedroom now."

"He's moving away, Syd! Great work! Thank you!"

Gotta hold the landline down, away from my mouth, and whisper into the cell: "Just get out of there, K. Now! Quick!"

"What about the drawer?"

"What drawer?"

"The drawer I broke. The lock snapped off. There were things inside, like, secret things I think. What should I . . ."

"Just get out, Keiko! Worry about it later. Call me once you're safe. Um, um, um . . . what's that, Franklin?" *Gotta hang up the cell, put the landline back to my ear, get my voice back to normal.* "I'm sorry, the reception got bad there for a minute."

"I said, Sydney, that I don't see any sign of a calendar anywhere. The place is a bit of a mess, though, and I didn't go through everything. I feel a little odd snooping through my wife's things. But it looks like she took a long time to pick out an outfit, even by Keiko standards. Expect a stunning ensemble when she arrives, wherever it is she's arriving."

What is he even saying? Sounds like he's trying to make a joke, but I'm not getting it because I'm worried about the broken desk drawer, which is probably what I should be worried about. What the heck am I going to do about that? Boy, I came up with a real Band-Aid of a plan, didn't I? When this really calls for stitches, and maybe some serious surgery. Whatever. So long as Keiko is out of that house, and safe.

"So, um, Sydney. I fail to see what else I can do for you, my dear. Looks like you'll just have to call her and confess. I'm sure she'll . . . wait a minute! Keiko? What are you . . ."

Oh, please no! He must have walked back into the living room and caught her!

"Well, welcome back, but what are you doing home, darling? And in, uh . . . sweatpants?" *What's that? She actually walked back into the house? When I just got her out of it? What on earth is she doing?* "No, I thought you were having breakfast with Sydney Bristow, actually. I have her on the phone here . . . what? Um, certainly. Uh, Sydney, I'm going to hand you over to my wife. Hold on a moment, will you?"

Calm down, Syd. Catch your breath.

"Hello, Sydney?"

"Keiko, what's going on? You have to get out of that house, right now, before he finds the broken drawer!"

What? Keiko's response to that is to laugh? Huh? "Oh, right, Syd! Breakfast! It completely slipped my mind!"

"What's going on, K? Do you not feel safe talking with him there?"

"I'd love to, Syd. Poached eggs and girl talk do sound good, but it's such a beautiful day. I was going to see if my husband wanted to come for a long walk with me. Would you be interested in that,

Franklin dear?" *Wow. Not bad, K. Buy us a little time, that way we can figure out a fix for the drawer. Impressive . . .* "Oh, I know you were planning on spending the morning working in that stuffy old office of yours. But look outside! It's incredible! As for Sydney, she's so used to me being late all the time, she'll be grateful for a straight-up cancellation for once. Right, Sydney?"

"Right, Keiko." *Gotta give it to her. The girl's smooth when she needs to be.*

"So you'll come? Fantastic, Franklin! Sydney, I'm going to pull my husband right out the door this very minute, and we'll be gone awhile. But I'll call you just as soon as we're back. Okay?" *Okay, K. Nice work.* "What's that, Franklin? Of course I have an appointment calendar! I'll show it to you another time. For now, um, just give me a minute to say good-bye to Sydney, and then we'll go. Um, Syd . . ." *She's lowering her voice:* "We'll walk to the beach and back, maybe farther. I should have him out for a few hours, easy. Thank you, by the way. I think you might have saved my life." *A scary thought. I've got to help this girl and get her out of this. But for now, she's raising her voice again:* "So take care, Sydney! Bye now!" *She's hung up. Well, that's that. Nicely handled.*

Sydney and Keiko: a pretty good team, it turns out.

Final note to self: Never marry a man you don't trust. What a terrible thing, to feel like you have to look through the desk of the person you love in order to know what's going on in his head! It must have been nearly impossible for Keiko to do that. It'd be hard even for a trained spy! Thank goodness I have something more solid than that with Michael. Look right there: his briefcase, sitting on the table. It'd be downright painful to open that up and start looking through it. How wonderful that that's something I'll never have to do!

Okay, okay. Enough thinking. We'll deal with the broken drawer. But for now, I'm going to reward myself with five more minutes of sleep. I deserve it. But wait: Did I just throw the cordless back on the counter without replacing it in the cradle? Oh, man. Michael really should talk to me about that later. . . .

CHAPTER 8

JUST OUTSIDE LAS VEGAS
THAT SAME DAY

The door opened, a bell rang, and a dry, dusty wind blew in some of the loose sand from the desert. Several men, all clad in overalls, glanced out from stooped positions over the open hoods of battered old cars to eyeball the two cowboys stepping into the mechanic's shop. One was older, weathered, with a grey stubble covering his chin and a cold look about him. The younger one was stockier, square-jawed and chatty, and his eyes darted about the room like he was anxious to look at some vintage machinery. Both were duded up in very different ways, the older man in a suit and a sharp bolo tie, and the younger in well-worn jeans and a T-shirt that rudely invited female passersby to SAVE A HORSE, RIDE ME.

"Aw, would ya look at this one, Pops!" exclaimed the younger man, tipping up his Stetson and bending down excitedly to inspect a beauty of an automobile in for refurbishing. "It's a sixty-six Corvair, with the original rear-mounted, air-cooled engine! Some of the upholstery could use work, and I'm guessin' the belts aren't perfect, but look at these lines! This one would be the best birthday present since you got me that little island a couple years back, the one in the Caribbean." He pronounced it "car-ribbon."

The younger man was almost salivating over the car. The older fellow, who didn't look much like his son, nodded and hitched up his belt. Some of the mechanics offered halfhearted greetings before turning back to their work. One mechanic, incongruously clad in a fishing hat complete with hooks and lures, wiped the oil off his right hand and held it out for the older man to shake, then proceeded to ignore the two cowboys for the rest of their visit. The mechanics had pretty much seen it all. With Paulson's Auto Body and Sales just a half hour from Vegas on I-15, the laborers didn't give a damn if some high roller and his lamebrain, car-loving son came in to look for a classic set of wheels. Even if, unbeknownst to them, the older man's name was Arvin Sloane, and the younger was Marshall Flinkman.

"Mah son here seems to have developed an abidin' interest in old automobiles," Sloane announced, with a thick twang coloring his voice.

"Paw tol' me, 'Son, you should pick yourself up one of them Maseratis or Ferraris or whatever they're callin' those dragsters nowadays,'" Marshall chimed in.

"Junior here's got a birthday comin', and his li'l heart is set on somethin' with character," Sloane offered.

"That's the very words I used. 'Somethin' with character.'" Marshall grinned like a pig in dirt. "I figure a car don't get character till it's been around awhile. I want a car that says to other cars, 'Hey, you think you're a car? Heck, you're just gettin' started bein' a car! Call me up in twenty, thirty years and we'll talk.' That is, y'know, if cars could use phones, or if we even continue usin' phones a couple decades down the line—"

"That'll do, son," Sloane said humorlessly.

"Aw, paw, never mind that Corvair! That there's a Fiat!" Marshall scrambled over to another car like a six-year-old who's spotted something shiny.

"Y'all feel like introducin' me to the proprietor of this establishment?" Sloane asked grandly to no one in particular. "I'd like to talk turkey over prices, if it's all the same to you."

Without removing his head from the hood of an old Camaro, the man sporting the fishing hat reached out and rapped a wrench on the window of the shop's office. "Arnie!" he called out. "Some folks want to speak to you!"

"Send 'em in!" came a gravelly voice from inside the office. Sloane strode in, his boots clacking sharply against the dirty concrete as he walked. Marshall continued flitting from car to car, genuinely enjoying the shop's impressive collection of old rides.

"Is this Camaro a seventy and a half?" Sloane heard Marshall ask excitedly as he stepped inside. "You've set it up for street and strip, huh? Nice!" As Sloane pulled the door shut behind him, silence fell over the cramped little office. It was ill-lit and covered in paperwork. Stacks of yellowing forms and ancient repair manuals sat unevenly atop overflowing filing cabinets. Arnold Paulson, a meek little man in a filthy flannel shirt, hunched over a transmission that had been unceremoniously dumped on his desk, fiddling at it ineffectively with a screwdriver.

"Be with you in just a minute," Paulson muttered, not looking up. "But feel free to have a seat." He glanced up to gesture toward a rickety folding chair. "Arvin, what a pleasure."

"Last we spoke, Arnold, you indicated a desire for discretion in future contact," Sloane said in his normal, accent-free voice. He grabbed a rag from Paulson's desk and used it to wipe the folding chair clean. "I imagine it's tough being completely off the espionage map, and I felt coming in disguise might make a visit from me more palatable." He tossed the rag aside and seated himself, folding his hands in his lap.

"I appreciate that," Paulson said, with a hint of uncertainty. "My employees don't know anything about my past, of course. But if they were to get the least bit suspicious, and if they saw me with any old contacts, well . . . They have loose lips, and that could be dangerous."

"Anything for an old acquaintance," Sloane said silkily, reaching into his jacket pocket and removing a vial of liquid. "I won't insult you by wasting your time. I'm here to ask you about this."

Paulson took the vial from him and turned it curiously in his hand. "It's saying something, you know, that I come to you when my own staff can't determine the chemical makeup of something. And I have a pretty solid team. But I've always said that you're the best chemist I've ever known."

"That's because I'm the best chemist there's ever been. I'd have a Nobel by now if the whole thing wasn't about politicking and favoritism." Paulson shook the vial vigorously, then held it near his ear and listened. "Just because a man's chemical achievements have, for the most part, been used for assassinations and terrorism doesn't make them any less impressive."

"Is it your fault none of your clients have found a way to make altruism profitable?" A sardonic twinge crept into Sloane's voice, but Paulson didn't notice.

"My thoughts exactly. So one pH-imbalanced truth serum leaves one agent in an asylum foaming at the mouth and blabbing every trade secret he can think of, and K-Directorate blackballs me for life. Is that fair?"

"I'd hire you myself, Arnold, if the CIA's rules

on background checks weren't so stringent. But for the moment," Sloane paused, watching Paulson uncap the vial and take a cautious whiff, "I need to know if you'll be able to break that down."

Paulson paused, as if thinking carefully, then resealed the vial and tossed it casually back to Sloane, who caught it with an expression of mild surprise at Paulson's cavalier gesture. "I don't need to analyze it," Paulson said with a broad, Cheshire-cat smile. "Because I made it."

Sloane sat silently, figuring Paulson would keep talking when he was ready. After a few seconds, however, it became clear that he was waiting for an acknowledgment of his brilliance, so Sloane finally deigned to offer a token murmur, one that Paulson decided to take for an expression of amazement.

"You see, Arvin," Paulson continued, "like you, the Kim brothers know who to call when they need someone who knows his way around a Bunsen burner. Now, my gifts are considerable—I'd go so far as to say I'm a veritable Santa's workshop full of gifts when it comes to assembling chemical compounds—but I still think creating that liquid, concocting it with almost nothing to base my research on, under tremendous deadline pressure . . . Well, it ranks easily among my top seven accomplishments. Ah, let's say top nine. But it wasn't easy. Not even for me."

Sloane's tongue moved over his lips, darting from corner to corner like a snake's. "I've no doubt it was quite the achievement. But perhaps you could tell me what the liquid actually is."

"I was basically playing detective. You know?" Paulson was speaking less to Sloane now than he was to some unseen admirer in his own imagination who was ravenous for every scrap of genius the great scientist had to offer. "I had my magnifying glass—though in this case it was a microscope—and my deerstalker cap—or, well, a white lab coat, anyway—and I tirelessly pursued the perpetrator of a deadly deed, never resting till I'd uncovered the truth! And keep in mind, it was not easy to break down the chemicals in the original formula."

Sloane sighed, rather loudly. It did little to stem the tide.

"So I had to ferret them out. But since I'm, you know, completely amazing, I coaxed them to justice. I truly am a wonder, I have to admit. But who wouldn't admit that? It's like all the ladies are always saying, 'Dr. P., you can break me down anytime,' which is kind of a funny chemistry joke. Not to make a pun on the idea of 'chemistry,' like the x-factor element in relationships, but sometimes my astonishing mind just makes these connections. . . ."

"I fear my own lesser mind might not be up to the task of discussing this with you, Arnold. Do you mind if I have my employee serve as a translator?"

Now it was Paulson's turn to sigh loudly, but Sloane had already risen and poked his head out the door of the office. "Son?" he called out.

"Yeah, paw?" came Marshall's cowboy voice. "Be right there!"

The sound of a closing hood and muttered thanks from Marshall to the mechanic who was showing him a pristine Gran Torino engine seeped into the room before Marshall himself appeared, closing the door behind him and making an unaccented introduction with a bright "Marshall Flinkman, sir. It's an honor to meet you. I've studied some of your work, and, while it is undoubtedly evil, it's really very clever, too."

"I'm told you're the man who needs to hear an explanation of this compound," Paulson sneered disdainfully, gesturing to the vial in Sloane's hands.

"Uh, yes, sir," Marshall said, pulling up the chair and leaving Sloane without a place to sit. "I tried all the usual techniques for analyzing its composition, but even the newest—the Strelchuk-Rosen protocols, which were just published in the journals last month, and the experimental Fontana serums that are still under CIA lock and key—got me nowhere. I've never seen anything like it."

Paulson seemed mildly impressed and softened his posture. "As the creator," Paulson said, leaning forward so that he and Marshall were facing each other, their faces mere feet apart, "I'm pleased to hear that my camouflage stood up to such careful scrutiny."

"You made that?" Marshall's eyes went wide, and he started gesticulating enthusiastically. "You've got to tell me how you did it!"

Paulson began to gesture wildly as well, as the two descended into jargon-filled effusions. It was like watching a science geek talk to himself in a mirror. "At its heart, you know, it's just basic recombinant org-chem, but I layered in a kind of chemical key, pulling out an electron from each nitrogen atom with a specific electrolyzer that has to be added, in reverse sequence, to any solvent you're adding for analytical purposes."

"Recombinant? So it's a biological neutralizer

with a lock-and-key concealment strain in the basic molecular structure. Incredible! That's brilliant!"

The two men really did seem to be getting on like gangbusters.

Sloane, however, feeling a bit left out of the joke, checked his watch. "Gentlemen, I hate to spoil the fun, but if you could focus on the matter at hand here, I'd appreciate it."

The laughter stopped. Paulson seemed put out at the prospect of dumbing down his complex scientific achievement so that it could be expressed in laymen's terms. Marshall smiled sympathetically, then attempted to mediate. "Well, Mr. Sloane, basically—and I hope I'm not oversimplifying here, Dr. Paulson, and forgive me if I am—but basically, if I'm hearing him right, the vial contains an antidote."

"Quite right," sniffed Paulson. "To the deadliest poison ever made."

The silence in the room suddenly felt oppressing.

LOS ANGELES
APO HEADQUARTERS

Vaughn poked his head into Jack's office. Jack looked up sharply, and Vaughn stepped in hesitantly when Jack gestured to a chair.

"Is there a problem, Agent Vaughn?"

"It's just . . ." He paused a moment, steeling himself. "It's just I don't know if I like keeping this information on Franklin Thornhill from Sydney. Jack, we don't even know what the connection means. I can't help feeling she'll be furious with us when she finds out." Vaughn blinked, feeling a little childish.

Jack's face was blank. "Are you questioning my decision to keep this intel on a strictly internal basis?"

"No, sir. I just . . ."

"And the director? You question Mr. Sloane's call to put her on suspension pending a full recovery from her injuries? An unfortunate side effect of which is leaving her out of the loop on internal investigations?"

Vaughn nodded an I-get-the-picture nod. "But Jack . . . we don't even know what the connection means."

Jack looked at him one last time, then looked back down at the work he'd been doing. The conversation was clearly over.

CHAPTER 9

LOS ANGELES THAT AFTERNOON

That Franklin Thornhill did not recognize the Anti-Ant Extermination Company van as being from a fictional company should not be taken as a mark of his intelligence or lack thereof. It was quite reasonable of him to assume, as he returned from a lengthy and tiring stroll with his wife, that the van parked outside his house and the somewhat portly man in a yellow jumpsuit waiting on his doorstep were both completely legit. And although, not having noticed any bug problem in his home previously, he was well within his rights to inquire of

Keiko whether she had called an exterminator, he was also a bit tired from his walk and anxious to move on with his day. Therefore, he failed to notice the long, suspicious preface in his wife's stammered-out explanation. "Oh, um, well, yes. Yes, I did." Franklin then awkwardly shook Eric Weiss's left hand and ushered the "exterminator" into his house.

"Must be tough, friend, zapping bugs with that arm in a sling," noted Franklin jauntily, helping Weiss lift a heavy, clanking bag apparently full of extermination equipment. "And having to work on a Sunday! You're having a rough week, I imagine."

"It sure is, buddy, and I sure am," Weiss responded. "But I took a little spill on a call out in Eagle Rock, and my shoulder got busted up. Shoulda seen the bugger that got me, though. Dampwood termite. Big as a house! If anyone ever tells you an exterminator's life is an easy one, don't believe them." Weiss paused, placing his hand over his heart, the look on his face indicating that the experience had been quite traumatic.

"Uh . . . Yes, well . . ." was the best response Franklin could come up with as Weiss collected himself, whipping out a fake work order and pretending to scrutinize it carefully. Keiko caught her husband's eye and shrugged.

"So, says here that you got a particular infestation in the—" Weiss spun in place, as if orienting himself against some sort of internal magnetic compass. "In the north wing of the house. That'd be, uh . . ." He spun some more, before pointing uncertainly toward Franklin's office. "That way, right?"

Before anyone could say a word, Weiss was already marching confidently toward the office, dragging his bag noisily behind him. Once inside, he unzipped the bag and began lifting out canisters and hoses, dropping them roughly all over the rug. Franklin and Keiko followed him in, unsure what to do. Weiss scanned the room with what seemed like a professional's eye, murmuring thoughtfully under his breath as if the office and its unwelcome insect inhabitants presented quite the thorny little problem.

"Yes, yes," he proclaimed finally. "Gonna have to spray in every nook and cranny in here. The li'l guys may be hiding, but I can still see them." He glanced at Keiko and Franklin. "If you don't mind, we're gonna have to close this room off for a bit. I don't want you breathing any toxic chemicals."

"Well, I'd intended to get some work done," Franklin hemmed, unsuccessfully masking his displeasure. "But I suppose if my wife says we have a bug problem, then we need to take care of it."

"Indeed, sir. Always listen to the missus, is the best policy."

"How about we'll leave you to it?" Franklin said.

"Oh, and I'll be needin' your John Hancock. Just an authorization form, y'know. . . ."

Playing the part of the exterminator to a T, Weiss flattened out the crumpled sheet he'd been holding, and Franklin grabbed a pen from the jar on his desk to sign. He paused, however, when he realized that he was holding the pen upside down. Keiko went sheet white. Weiss cocked his head in confusion, and a very long, very tense moment passed before Franklin finally turned the pen around slowly in his grip and signed the form. He seemed lost in reflection as he tucked the pen back in the jar, staring at it intently afterward.

"Thank you, sir," Weiss said brightly, clearing his throat in an effort to break the tension. "Now, if you'll just excuse me, it'll only take a few minutes to spray, but an artist hates to be disturbed, you know?" Franklin mustered a faintly preoccupied smile as he was ushered out the door, with Keiko stumbling just a little as she followed. Weiss shut the door behind them and locked it, exhaling with relief and slumping against the jamb.

"You comfortable out there, Syd?" he said softly.

"Snug as a bug," Sydney replied through the comm. Out in the van she adjusted her own earpiece delicately and twisted a few knobs on the surveillance console installed before her. "They've really improved the cushioning in these seats since the last time I was the communications relay. What do you need from me?"

"Nothing just yet," Weiss replied. He was checking the broken lock on the lower right desk drawer, nodding to himself as he realized how quickly Franklin would have noticed the damage if they hadn't come in to fix it. "But you'll be scratching my back in return before too long, Bristow. Only two reasons I'm here right now: I need your help scoping out Nadia's feelings, and *TPIR* isn't on on weekends."

"You're referring to it with an acronym now?"

"Those of us in the know, we have our jargon, Syd."

Sydney laughed, listening to Weiss riffle through the pages of an APO report on locks and keys. She'd done similar work enough times to recognize each individual sound in the process: the series of clinks as Weiss weighed each of the possible replacement locks he'd brought against the broken original, looking for a perfect match; the delicate whirr of an electric screwdriver ejecting the lock couplings, the *zip-zip-zip* of the sander removing any trace of damage to the drawer itself, and the wet squish and sizzle of Weiss using APO key-replicating equipment to clone the tiny teeth of the lock in the original drawer and duplicate it in the replacement.

"Bear with me, Syd. A guy's sleight-of-hand is slower when one's in a sling."

"You're doing great, Eric. Now place those bugs and get back out here."

"There'll be one in every nook and cranny, as we exterminators say. But for now I'm signing off to minimize reception interference while I set up the mikes. I had to grab some bottom-of-the-barrel mikes, since I'm technically on leave, and these interfere pretty severely with our earpiece comms. Hang on a sec, okay?"

Sydney leaned back and took a sip from her cup of coffee. She watched a series of red lights begin to flash as each of the microphones Weiss was installing went online. The sophisticated listening equipment created a three-dimensional sonic representation of Keiko and Franklin's house.

In Sydney's ears the tiny but unmistakable noises of the office fell into place one by one: Weiss's feet as they fell against the carpet; the ticking of a clock on one wall; the scrape of Franklin's golf trophy being moved aside as Weiss affixed a bug; even a gentle whirring as Franklin's computer idled. Then more sensitive mikes began picking up sounds through the walls: a faint hum from a lamp in the central living room; a louder drone from a fan set up to circulate air through the house. And Sydney could even hear, two rooms away, Franklin and Keiko talking in the kitchen.

"—which is why you could have told me," Franklin was saying. From a soft scraping sound, Sydney deduced that he was spreading something on toast. "You know I don't like to have other people in my office."

Keiko replied in such a soft, meek voice that Sydney couldn't make out her response.

"Bugs!" Franklin scoffed. "I've never seen a single one. But if they've started breeding in here, it's because you don't work hard enough to keep the place clean. Maybe if you spent a little less time running up my credit card bill with Sydney . . ."

Keiko answered again. This time a few words, punctuated by sobs, made their way through. ". . . she's my friend . . . while Dad's been hard to reach . . . be more understanding . . ."

"No one," Franklin said coldly, "is more aware of your dad's silence than I am."

The conversation disappeared in a deafening roar of electronic squeals, and Sydney quickly turned down one mike after another until only Weiss was audible. "I thought you were going offline to avoid feedback, Eric!"

"Sydney," his voice came through the comm, sounding very serious, "I need to show you something."

"Bring it out here when you're done, Eric. I can't talk now!" She turned Weiss off completely and tuned back in to Franklin and Keiko's conversation. She heard Weiss awkwardly bid them farewell, assuring them that their house would be roach-free henceforth and that his bill would be forthcoming. A tense silence followed the slamming of the door.

"Well . . . ," seethed Franklin, leaving the word hanging like a threat as he headed for his office. Sydney listened to his footsteps leading down the hall, softening as he hit the rug and stepped around his desk to tug sharply at the locked desk drawer, testing it. Sydney sighed with relief, trying not to think about what might have happened to Keiko if he'd seen the drawer twenty minutes earlier.

"Keiko!" she heard him call after he'd spent a few minutes on the computer. *Why didn't we install an e-mail duplicator on his desktop?* she scolded herself. *This is what comes from doing the op-tech yourself, instead of running it by Marshall.* "Come in here. I have a task for you."

The door of the van opened and Weiss appeared, a serious look on his face. Sydney held up one finger to tell him to wait.

"Yes, Franklin?" Keiko could be heard saying.

"Tomorrow you need to pick up a package at the post office. It's from China, addressed to you. But—and this is very important—you must not open it under any circumstances."

Could you be any less subtle? Sydney thought.

"You do understand what I'm saying, right? Do not open it." Sydney could hear Keiko whimpering a little. Whatever Franklin was doing, it was scaring her. *Okay,* Sydney decided, *that's enough.* She pulled off the headset and began to rise to go in and protect her friend, but Weiss grabbed her arm, stopping her. "Sydney, I think this is more complicated than you realize."

"We'll discuss that when I get back," Sydney said shortly.

Weiss didn't let her go. "I looked in the drawer after I replaced the lock. I saw what was inside."

"Keiko said there were surveillance photos."

"Yes," Weiss said. "And there's a connection here we didn't know about. Did she tell you who they were photos of?"

He placed the pictures he'd taken from the drawer on the console, and Sydney drew in her breath sharply. She didn't need to reply in the negative. After all, never having met him, how could Keiko have possibly known these were pictures of Jack Bristow?

CHAPTER 10

WASHINGTON, D.C.
DAYS LATER

CIA TELEPHONE SURVEILLANCE REPORT
Pentagon Station, Code #5191, Building 23
Submitted by Operative B. Oropallo, ID#11-06

Per recent directive (authorization: ARVIN SLOANE), by which all international mobile and land telephone conversations containing mention of key APO personnel are to be flagged and monitored, a recording was placed in archive.

The call was made from a remote APO listening outpost, triangulated to a suburban street in Manhattan Beach, California, to a mobile phone in Tokyo, Japan. Initiated by Agent SYDNEY BRISTOW and received by Agent NADIA SANTOS, the call has been carefully scanned for sensitive information and determined to fall within acceptable bounds for interagent communication. Recommendation: NO FURTHER ACTION NECESSARY.

For the purposes of record, a brief synopsis and select transcriptions follow:

Agent BRISTOW (hereafter referred to as "SB") telephoned Agent SANTOS ("NS") to express worry about the safety of her father, Agent JACK BRISTOW ("JB"). Conversation excerpt begins at recording point 00:01:46.

NS: . . . no, and I'm sorry, but I haven't seen him, Syd. He's been off the grid all afternoon, and I don't expect to run into him again until our rendezvous this evening. But that's pretty typical, right? I mean, who knows where the guy spends his free time?

SB: I just think he ought to know about this. I mean, these pictures were locked in this man's desk drawer. I already had a bad feeling about Franklin, and now . . .

NS: But they're just pictures, right?

SB: Surveillance photos. Of my dad chasing a man, subduing him, then pursuing him when he gets away. There are even a couple of the car my dad jumps into, driving off. I don't know who it is, when they were taken, anything. . . .

NS: Well, they certainly don't seem like anything he needs to worry about. Your dad has faced far worse than some lab technician armed with a telephoto lens.

SB: I suppose so. It's just . . . something's not right here.

NS: Seems to me it can wait until after our meet tonight. After all, what's this Franklin Thornhill going to do? Paddle all the way across the Pacific and ambush your dad? Stop worrying about it. . . . (Excerpt ends at recording point 00:02:38.)

A short discussion of NS and JB's current mission followed. In speaking to SB, NS skirted agency protocol on the discussion of mission particulars with suspended agents, but the details revealed are almost certainly noncompromising to ongoing APO activities. Transcript continues from 00:05:57.

NS: Yeah. I think the blue is probably the one. It's showy, but sometimes in order to blend in, you have to stand out a little.
SB: This is for a meet?
NS: Yes. With a Japanese arms financier who, I hear, likes his ladies on the Latin side. Which is creepy, but you have to use what you've got. . . .

NOTE: The financier mentioned here, according to APO internal documents, is KIYOAKI HONDA, a well-known associate of FAN LI KIM, thought to be a crucial financial link between the Kim brothers (FAN LI and EDDIE, the latter recently deceased) and the DARK CLOUD SECT. Further investigation is necessary to determine the extent of the theorized link. However, it is worth noting that no further investigation need be made into NS's assertion of Honda's fondness for South American women, which is well documented. (See CIA Proclivities Report #481-5162, with particular reference to Buenos Aires Station Code #342. Note that this material is what some might term "Not Safe for Work.") Transcript continues:

NS: We really need to get to him. We're not much closer to stopping these guys than we were in Kuala Lumpur.
SB: Just keep an eye on my dad. I know he can handle himself, but, you know, a storm can blow up out of nowhere sometimes. And this is one he doesn't know is coming.
NS: So, uh . . . If I'm hearing you right, you're saying get the blue. Are you sure? Because now I'm thinking maybe the black. . . . (Excerpt ends at 00:06:20.)

Laughter and banter followed. Eventually SB broached the topic of NS's relationship with Agent Eric Weiss ("EW"). Let it be noted that SB seemed somewhat uncomfortable with the subject. Transcript continues from 00:08:24.

SB: You two seem to be growing really close. I thought my time off from work would be you and me hanging around the house, Nadia, but you're always off with Eric. Not that I'm upset. I'm just curious whether I should be looking for a new roommate.
NS: Michael seems more than capable of doing the shopping when you don't feel up to it, Syd, and he pretty much lives with us already.
SB: So that means you're planning on taking things to the next level?
NS: Sydney! (Excerpt ends at 00:08:43.)

The insinuating tone of SB's inquiries into "the next level" might alarm some, but there is no indication that the agents were speaking in code. Searches of CIA and APO databases for espionage-related operations code-named "The Next Level" yielded one aborted nation-building project in central Asia from the mid-1980s, as well as some references to mind-control-through-video-games programs from a decade later. None of this seems related to the matter at hand, and this analyst feels certain the term was nothing more than a euphemism for accelerating the emotional progress of a romantic relationship. The conversation included nothing more pertinent to APO, its personnel, or its operations, and concluded with the standard farewells at 00:13:38.

ADDITIONAL NOTE #1: Pains have been taken to make this report highly detailed. It is expected that investigations will have to be made into the alarming events that took place in a Japanese hostess bar subsequent to this call, and the recording may prove useful in deciding what went wrong with the NS/JB operation.

ADDITIONAL NOTE #2: A second call, placed by NS to EW's cell phone immediately after this one, contains even less noteworthy material. (Repeated iterations of "No, *you* hang up" seem irrelevant to CIA or APO affairs.) But as EW seems to have been sitting next to SB in the APO listening van when the call was placed—a fact that may explain SB's audible unease at discussing her sister's romantic affairs—careful sonic analysis from that call yields some further background detail that seems worthy of inclusion in this report. It seems SB was examining some documents—the photographs referred to in excerpt 00:01:46–00:02:38, presumably—and on this second call she can be overheard talking softly to herself as she considers them. Her musings are recorded below:

SB: Something seems familiar about these pictures. . . . I feel like I recognize the place where they were taken, but everything other than my dad is blurry and hard to make out. What are these odd gray shapes behind him? Could they be in a cemetery?

CHAPTER 11

DAYS EARLIER
TOKYO

Jack Bristow was not the sort of man you'd expect to find sitting in a cramped noodle shop in a seedy back alley not far from Tokyo's Shinjuku Station. But then this wasn't the sort of noodle shop where people go to be found, and the other patrons, shady characters one and all in stark contrast to Jack's natty tailoredness, paid Jack the courtesy of not noticing him in exchange for his ignoring them in turn. It was quiet, and it was hot, fifteen Japanese men squeezed into a space fit for ten, all hunched over steaming bowls of ramen sizzling with pork grease, everyone nervously waiting for something or other. Most of these somethings or other were of questionable legality at best, and more than a few of them would end very badly. The patrons seemed aware of that and at peace with it, and content to eat what might be their last meal alone in this sad little place.

Jack checked his watch idly, swirling his barely touched noodles with his chopsticks. It was almost time. He tossed a thousand-yen note and a couple of hundred-yen coins down on the counter, muttered the customary "*Gochisousama*"—"Thank you for the meal"—and made his way past a roomful of averted eyes to the front door. Just outside the shop was a green public pay phone, a staple of every Japanese public thoroughfare and subject to surprisingly regular use despite the popularity of cell phones.

These things will still be here when all of us are gone, Jack thought with some satisfaction as he fished in his pocket for a cheap, untraceable plastic phone card. *Some things fade away, while others endure forever. Strange how that works.*

He checked his watch again. The second hand was creeping toward the twelve. Jack looked around to be sure no one was watching or listening, and he began dialing the long international number. He paused before the last digit until the second hand swept past its zenith, then pressed and waited while the uniquely Japanese burbling ring sounded in his ear. Suddenly it stopped.

LONDON

Arvin Sloane was exactly the sort of man for whom airport waiting lounges are made, and he looked completely at ease. But then the elite lounge at London's Heathrow Airport was built for comfort, and everyone in the room, powerful men in businesses no less insidious or ruthless than Sloane's, relaxed in cushy chairs as they sipped fizzy drinks and perused newspapers that had been ironed that morning to a crisp flatness by uniformed stewards. Music was playing on hidden speakers at a volume so low that the passengers-to-be couldn't be sure they weren't imagining it, and everyone was unanxiously whiling away the time before a flight to some exotic place—Dubai, or Bangalore, or Chicago—where they would get down to work and promptly forget that this waiting lounge even existed. Crossed-legged postures, idly puffed cigars, and occasional inquiries into time differences were the order of the day.

Sloane drank the last of his tea, glanced up at the master clock in the center of the room, and waved his hand for an attendant to remove the remnants of an elderberry scone. It was almost time. He stood, dusting himself off needlessly, and strolled over to a small bank of pay phones at the rear of the room. No one used these any longer, so prevalent were mobile phones and Blackberries among the power elite, and Sloane imagined that if the lounge weren't so assiduously cleaned, so regularly, he might very well still be able to detect the smudge of his own fingerprints on the handset from the last time he'd stood here.

One day they'll get rid of these obsolete old machines, he thought to himself. *They'll just decide it's not worth maintaining them any longer. But for now, they still have their purpose.*

Another look at the clock indicated that he should be ready. His hand hovered over the receiver in anticipation as the clock turned over another minute, and then the phone suddenly began to ring. Sloane smiled, admiring the precision, and picked up.

TOKYO

There was silence for a moment before Jack heard Sloane's familiar voice on the other end. "Your timing is perfect, as always," Sloane said, a false brightness failing to mask his trademark rasp.

"The benefits of buying a quality watch," Jack responded tersely.

"I was thinking," responded Sloane airily, "as I was catching that flight out of McCarran earlier today, and listening to the clanging and ringing of the slot machines in the terminal, that there are times when life is too full of noise and complication. Sometimes a man yearns for the simpler things, like a prearranged pay phone rendezvous with a contact on the other side of the world. Unbuggable, untraceable, and utterly satisfying as a piece of well-coordinated espionage work. It's nice to fall back on protocols established long ago with old friends."

Jack couldn't help thinking wryly that he was glad Sloane was enjoying himself. *This cloak-and-dagger routine means a lot of unnecessary legwork and an unwelcome period of going completely dark,* he thought with a grimace, and none of it would be necessary if Sloane himself hadn't instituted communications monitoring triggered by any mention of APO personnel. Even this conversation had to include no names. It was ridiculous.

LONDON

It was always hard to say what exactly gave Arvin Sloane pleasure, but if pressed, he himself would probably say "control." That he could make a man he respected and even, within limits, trusted as much as Jack Bristow follow a fresh-off-the-Farm CIA routine like this phone call gave him a strange thrill. It also kept this status report off the books, which was sometimes an advantage. And Sloane was a man who always liked having the advantage.

"Much as I relish discussing the simple joys of a street telephone," Jack said, willing himself not to say Sloane's name, "I would prefer to hear where we stand in our investigations of Dark Cloud." The name of the organization, Jack remembered, was deemed too generic to have been included in the bugging process.

"I've tracked down a sample of an antidote to a deadly poison that I think we can presume Dark Cloud plans to disseminate as part of its attack. We're still determining the nature of the poison itself, but an entire building in Alexandria, Virginia, stands ready to produce the antidote in bulk in the event of a strike."

"Which we still hope to avert, I assume."

"Of course," Sloane said.

"And yet we still don't know the nature or the location of the target. Can we hazard a guess that the poison will be sprayed directly onto agricultural fields or maybe into a reservoir? It would explain the rumor that crop dusters are involved."

"Perhaps. It's even possible the plan is to spray the poison directly onto a population, since it appears the toxics pass through the skin."

"The fear, in that case," Jack reasoned, "would be that Dark Cloud is considering a preliminary run using the dusters, with an eye toward utilizing a more sophisticated delivery system in the future."

"I agree. I've just completed a visit with a contact here in London, which sadly proved fruitless, but I intend to resume my inquiries after I return to Los Angeles on the next flight. It's amazing what you can turn up, just by going through your address book and ringing up old acquaintances."

"Indeed."

"And speaking of old friends, I hear your erstwhile

number two man from your Venezuela days has come back into your life, in a sense."

TOKYO

Jack clenched his teeth slightly. Wanting to deal with it—if it needed dealing with at all—on his own, he had hoped to keep this matter from Sloane. But it was not at all unlikely that the very conversation in which he had attempted to contain the information—by forbidding Vaughn to tell Sydney about the strange connection—had been bugged. He sighed, nodding a little and pressing on.

LONDON

Sloane's eyes wandered across the room and fell upon a man in sleek pinstripes watching him a little too carefully. Sloane took the face and ran it through his mental archive, adding glasses or changing the hairstyle, and started slightly when he decided the man looked most familiar in a fishing hat. *But this can't be the mechanic from Paulson's*, he thought, shaking his head and dismissing the idea.

"A member of our organization was asked, as a favor, to look into the husband of a friend of my daughter's. It turns out this Franklin Thornhill is the son of Roger Thornhill, my old associate. . . ."

"And a man you killed in an off-the-books operation in New Orleans six years ago, if I'm not mistaken." The very matter-of-factness of Sloane's tone was a kind of jab—he knew that this was one of the few killings ever to give Jack pangs of guilt.

"Roger was an unfortunate casualty of fatherly protectiveness."

"It seems an odd coincidence, doesn't it? Do you think his son is aware that his wife is connected to his father's killer?"

"If Franklin were targeting me, or even trying to hurt me by targeting my daughter, there are more effective ways to get revenge than by marrying one of her friends." Jack paused. It wasn't quite that simple, he knew. "Nevertheless . . ."

"You're uneasy about it. I don't blame you. Men in our profession don't get to be where we are by dismissing our investigative instincts. But without any evidence that this Franklin Thornhill even knows the identity of his father's killer, we have to assume . . ."

"We assume nothing," Jack cut him off. "I will put people in place to keep an eye on the situation.

In the meantime we need to focus on Dark Cloud. Tonight's meet with Kiyoaki Honda will either shed some light on things or leave us back at square one."

"Question him carefully. And . . . be insistent if you need to."

Jack's eyes fell on something nearby and his voice grew more distant. "I know how to ask forcefully, if it comes to that. Hold on a moment, will you?"

TOKYO

Jack had noticed an unshaven man in a heavy jacket—despite the oppressive Tokyo heat—loitering near him for a little longer than seemed necessary. Jack offered him a smile, which seemed to fill the scruffy man with confidence, and he sauntered over toward Jack's phone.

With a lightning-quick movement, Jack whipped the phone cord around the man's neck, pulling it just tight enough to pin him gaspingly in place. The man tried to yell, but couldn't get enough air through his throat.

LONDON

Sloane grunted agreement and pretended to examine his fingernails idly. All the while his eyes snuck glances at the suspicious pinstriped man across the room.

It's not impossible to imagine there's an ex-K-Directorate watchman in Paulson's shop, Sloane found himself thinking, *but to send him here to follow me seems a bit extreme.*

Suddenly he heard a strangled cry through the earpiece—not an entirely unusual thing to hear during a conversation with Jack Bristow—and his attention returned to the phone.

TOKYO

"Forgive me, just a minor interruption," Jack said, his face very close to the scruffy man's as he spoke into the phone whose cord wrapped around the man's windpipe.

"Not at all," Sloane replied, eyeballing the pinstriped man and letting his lip curl in a tiny sneer. "It's your dime, as they say."

Jack patted the man down and heard the telltale clink of metal. He pulled the heavy jacket open and found, to his astonishment, an array of wristwatches and jewelry—knockoffs, all of it—hanging from tiny hooks on the jacket's lining.

"Want to buy," croaked the man in English even more strained by the cord around his neck, "cheap Rolex?"

Jack grimaced, and let him go.

LONDON

Sloane impulsively caught the man's eye and waved him over. The man seemed surprised but walked closer inquisitively.

"Do you have the time?" Sloane whispered to him, holding up his watch. "I've lost track of the difference between here and New Delhi."

With a polite nod, the man told him and left, not noticing the click of the camera on Sloane's wrist.

"Sorry about that," Jack said back into the phone. "Little misunderstanding between me and a passerby."

"It happens to all of us. I'll let you get to your meet," Sloane said, pressing the buttons on his watch to send the photo back to APO headquarters. "But, um . . ." He paused, uncharacteristically, either distracted or moved by some tiny emotion. "Watch out for my daughter, will you?"

Jack nodded understandingly. "Of course. I know you'd do the same for me."

CHAPTER 12

HOURS LATER
LOS ANGELES

"So, how's life at the bank?"

Sydney looked up from where she was adjusting the wire on the inside of Keiko's blazer. She half-expected Keiko to be sporting an excited grin, but instead her friend was wide-eyed, unreadable. Sydney blinked twice, but Keiko's expression didn't change. "It's good," Sydney assured her flatly, before getting back to the wire.

"Been doing a lot of . . . banking?"

Sydney looked up once again. "I'm kind of in the middle of this, K. We want to be able to hear in case anything goes wrong. Not that anything will. We're just being safe."

"Sure, sure. Sorry. I guess I'm a little nervous." Keiko didn't sound nervous. In fact, she sounded kind of energized. Ever since Sydney had suggested her plan, Keiko was all abuzz, like a child on a sugar high. Even now she couldn't sit still, and she'd fumbled with attaching the wire so many times that in the end Sydney simply knelt down to do it for her, like a mom helping a child with an untied shoe. "Plus, lately I'm sort of curious about, you know, the bank trade."

Sydney finished attaching the wire, giving it a tug to be sure it was fixed firmly, and turned her eyes up to gaze hard into Keiko's face, her lips pursed. Then she smiled, and Keiko smiled back. "You know my favorite thing about banks, Keiko?"

"What's that?"

"They're secure. You put your money in, and you know it'll be safe."

Keiko bit her lip. "I suppose, if it weren't safe to put money in a bank, people would just . . . I dunno . . . they'd hide it under their mattresses."

Sydney nodded. "Exactly."

"Or stuff it in old shoeboxes, or wear it in those belts under their clothes."

"Right."

Keiko looked down at her lap, thinking for a moment. "I wouldn't want to wear one of those belts," she mused aloud. "It'd make me look flabby. Unless, maybe, I could get one that you wear on top," she added brightly, looking up and waving one hand vaguely over her bosom. "I could use a little more bulk here. I don't really have a lot goin' on up top."

With an amused shake of the head, Sydney patted Keiko twice on the knee and stood up.

"Time to get to work?" Keiko asked. Sydney nodded, and Keiko rose as well, smoothing out her jacket. The wire was invisible. She seemed pleased. A banker's work," she sighed, "is never done."

Sporting sunglasses and plain clothes, Weiss stood outside the van, which was now painted a nondescript brown, and peered carefully up and down the street. He reached back and banged his fist a couple of times against the vehicle's metal door. "All clear out here," he said, and with a sliding clang Keiko emerged into the sunlight, squinting as she shaded her eyes with her arm. Weiss helped her step down. He couldn't help noticing the eerie lack of a nervous shake in her hand as he held her steady. Either this girl had nerves of steel, or she was a natural at the spy game. *Or,* he realized, *it's possible she has no idea what she's getting into.*

"Ready to do this, Keiko?"

"I think so," she said, her eyes adjusting to the brightness. "Hey, another exterminator," she added distantly, gesturing to a second van down the street.

Weiss chuckled. "There've been vans all up and down the block. It happens. People see our van parked outside a house, get paranoid there might be bugs in their place, and call a real exterminator of their own. I should remember to buy stock in Orkin just prior to one of our operations."

"That's thinking like a banker," Keiko said, then pointed at the side of the other van. "Ever heard of Mosquito Bandito Exterminators?"

Weiss thought for a moment, then demurred. "Not really something I, uh, pay much attention to."

"Neither have I," Keiko concurred without listening. She seemed to brush a thought aside, then continued, "Do we need to check whether this thing's working, or . . ." She tapped gently on her jacket, indicating the wire.

Weiss leaned in. "Testing, testing . . . Syd, can you hear?"

"No need to get quite so close to her chest, Eric," came Sydney's teasing voice from inside the van. "We're picking up just fine."

Weiss seemed abashed. "I wasn't . . . ," he began, haltingly. Keiko was chuckling, enjoying his embarrassment. "I, uh . . . I happen to be spoken for, so . . ."

"You remember the plan, K?" Sydney interrupted, poking her head out into the sun.

"Yes, Sydney. We've been over it a thousand times. . . ."

Keiko stepped off the bus and hurried down the street toward the post office. Downtown Manhattan Beach was a cute little area, full of ritzy shops and stiff-postured people walking immaculately groomed dogs. It was one of those rare places where teenagers dressed in surfwear actually knew how to surf, and where people regularly took their Vespas out to pick up their groceries at the Ralphs. It had been a long time since the town had seen intrigue more complex than a clumsy effort to keep a loved one from noticing an exorbitant charge on a credit card statement. As Keiko strode briskly down the old-fashioned little street, no one could have guessed what she was up to. She felt like she was becoming adept at the spy game. Practice made perfect, plus she had been well coached. It was obvious that Sydney and Weiss weren't really bankers, and she knew she was in good hands. There would be a time and a place for asking questions.

"I'm going to be doing what you guys call a drop-dead," Keiko had recited stiffly in response to Sydney's request to go over the plan once more, just to be safe.

"A dead-drop," corrected Weiss. "And if you stick to the plan, it's pretty much guaranteed to go smoothly. Sydney and I have done a thousand of these."

"Of course." Keiko nodded. "Apparently it's a skill you learn your first week in the bank business."

Weiss looked confused, but Sydney and Keiko just blinked innocently. A lightbulb went on over his head. "Oh! Oh, I get it. The bank business. So we're sticking with that?"

"For now," said Sydney.

"Cool."

"Anyway," Keiko had continued, "before I get to the actual dead-dropping, first I have to pick up the package at the post office. . . ."

The line at the counter was long and moved like molasses. "You could just get the American flag ones like everybody else," Keiko found herself muttering impatiently under her breath as an old lady fussed over whether to buy stamps with flowers or birds on them. Keiko's repeated checking of her watch wasn't born out of nervousness so much as a burning desire to keep this little operation moving.

That man over there has been filling out his change-of-address form for an awfully long time, she thought. *And is it just my imagination, or has he been sneaking glances at me? I'm a good-looking girl, no doubt, but today is not the day to be showing an interest in Keiko, buddy.* She decided to deal with the matter head-on and stared openly at him until he glanced at her again. The man started when his eyes met her cold, daggerlike stare, then he gathered up his things and beat a hasty retreat out the door. Keiko tried not to be too pleased with herself as she finally reached the head of the line, showed her driver's license, and waited for the clerk to bring her the package.

". . . and once I have it," she'd gone on at Sydney and Weiss's urging, "I need to carry it outside, holding it in plain view so you guys can see what it looks like and duplicate it. I don't think I even want to know how you're going to do that."

"It's less high-tech than you'd think," Weiss had said. "And sadly, I'm guessing it's gonna wind up being my job. . . ."

Weiss sat in the unmarked car, surrounded by the coffee-stained and dog-eared detritus of a hundred boring stakeouts and scanning for signs that Keiko was being watched. A couple of dudes who seemed a little too shady for the surroundings got his antennae up, but he eventually decided they were probably just beach bums who'd wandered up from the water. He saw a man scramble out of the post office while Keiko was inside, but that guy didn't seem like a threat either.

"I think we're all set, Syd," Weiss whispered into a tiny mike.

In the van, Sydney heard Weiss over the comm, as she heard Keiko thanking the post office clerk for bringing her the package. "It sounds like she's on her way out, Eric."

"Copy that." Weiss watched as Keiko emerged from the post office, twirling the package idly in her hands as she walked leisurely down the street. The *clickety-click* of the camera shutter sent photos of the package into the laptop open on the passenger seat, and Weiss got to work, mumbling to himself as he did so: "Brown paper, Chinese postage, looks to be about two inches by five by seven. . . ." *I must have something in here that's the perfect size,* he thought as he rummaged through the bric-a-brac on the dashboard. *Aha! That'll do nicely!* Once he'd found a shape match, a case in the backseat provided all the necessary materials to wrap it up and reproduce the package perfectly. A tiny printer even produced a duplicate of the address label, which Weiss attached to the package. "Syd, I'd say we're good to go."

". . . you're in excellent hands. Or hand," Weiss had said, holding up his one unbroken arm. Keiko had given this a polite smile before moving on.

"So our goal," she had said, all business, "is going to be switching the real package with the fake one, without anyone noticing, long enough for you to open the real one up and decide what to do with the contents."

"Right," Sydney had said. "We'll copy whatever we can, corrupt anything dangerous, and evaluate the dangers of passing the package along to Franklin. Whatever we decide to give him, we'll seal back up and make another switch before you get home."

"And you do remember," Weiss quizzed her, "how to go about the actual dead-drop, right?"

Keiko had been very patient, taking a deep breath before explaining that part of the plan yet again: "Yes. I'm going to take the package down the street, where I'll pick up the duplicate from you just after tossing the real package into the trash can at the corner of Manhattan Beach and Morningside Drive. . . ."

"Sydney, I think we have a problem," Keiko said, stopping in her tracks just short of Morningside.

"I see it, K," Sydney said to no one in particular, pulling the van into a spot not far from where Keiko was standing. She'd decided not to give Keiko an earpiece, thinking it might throw her off since she wasn't used to having someone speak in her ear. Now, however, she wished she had a way to communicate with her.

A traffic accident at the appointed dead-drop corner had sent a white BMW convertible careening up onto the sidewalk, flattening the trash can in question against the concrete of an apartment building garage. Fast-food wrappers and Big Gulp cups oozed out of the can's distended sides, and police officers milled about taking down details from eyewitnesses. Keiko stood, staring at the wreck, hemming and hawing a little as she decided what to do.

"You havin' some trouble, ma'am?" came a voice from nearby, startling Keiko considerably. She turned to find a female police officer, directing traffic around the accident, looking curiously her way.

"Oh, no, Officer. I was just going to throw this out," Keiko stammered, holding up the package. "In that trash can."

The policewoman turned to look at the squashed bin. "Maybe you'd better move along. I'm sure you'll find another place to dispose of it." She waved on a massive pickup truck that was waiting to squeeze past the parked black-and-white cars. Keiko continued to stand there, apparently stunned.

Come on, K, Sydney thought to herself while adjusting a blond wig on her head and straightening the pins on her lapel. She cracked open her mascara. *Part of doing this is being able to think on your feet. You can do it, I know it.*

"Looks like Keiko's stumbling," Weiss said, concerned. He pulled a mail carrier uniform out of the backseat.

"She'll pull it together," Sydney said with a hint of uncertainty. "This is a minor hiccup, and she knew we had a plan B in case something like this happened." Sometimes, Sydney knew, inexperienced people gave mere lip service to the backup plan, never figuring they'd have to use it, and even with a good secondary scenario in place, ops often went awry when some tiny unexpected element entered the mix. Sydney watched Keiko shifting her weight uneasily, apparently withering under the watchful glare of the policewoman.

". . . but if for some reason I can't put it in the trash can, I drop it in the mailbox a block farther down," Keiko had recited.

"Well, then, let's get this show on the road." Sydney had grinned, patting Keiko on the back reassuringly, grabbing her cane, and hobbling back to the van's front seat. There she checked to make sure her backup costume was all laid out, complete

with the wig and the pins on the lapel. Hopefully she wouldn't have to use it. She had watched Keiko head for her bus, and then she and Weiss, in separate vehicles, had headed off toward the rendezvous point downtown.

"If you want, miss, you could toss that out in the Dumpster right over there." Keiko didn't seem to understand, so the officer nodded her head toward the large metal crate peeking out from around the corner of an apartment building that was under construction. The officer was clearly doing her best to pretend to be patient. "It all winds up in the same place, provided you dispose of it properly. And in a timely fashion," she added pointedly.

Keiko hesitated, turning the package in her hand. *Why shouldn't I throw this in the Dumpster? I could do that and be done with all this. If Sydney and Eric are watching me like they said they would be, they'll see where I put it and it won't matter which garbage can, right? But wait—I need to put it in the right place because I need to be in the right place to pick up the fake package really quickly, in case Franklin's watching me too. Is Franklin watching? Is anyone?* For the first time since it had begun to dawn on Keiko exactly what Sydney did for a living, she started to feel nervous. The policewoman's eyes were so heavy on her that she suddenly became aware of the other eyes ostensibly tracking her every move: Sydney's and Weiss's, plus the sinister man with the change-of-address form, and there could be other people looking out of each of the windows in every car and building on the street. Franklin, with those eyes of his that seemed like they saw everything, could be anywhere. . . . Keiko started to panic. *I have to get out of here, find someplace to sit, and think carefully about this. What if it's all in my mind? What if I was just looking for a little excitement in my life and cooked up this crazy my-husband-is-a-spy thing and it got out of hand? Maybe the package is nothing, maybe the desk drawer is nothing, maybe Franklin's just a little rough with me because, like he says, he loves me so much. . . .*

Sydney watched as Keiko turned and started away from the crumpled trash can, moving farther from the mailbox as well. *No, no, no!* Sydney urged her in her mind. *Come back to us, K. You can do this. I know it's easy to lose focus when things go wrong. But you have to stay on task: We need that package.* For the first time, Sydney understood the anxiety Vaughn must have felt each time he sent her out on a mission while she was at SD-6. *I wonder if I ever realized back then just how hard his job was,* she thought absently as she hopped out of the car, testing out her weight on her leg and finding that, though she was shaky, she could stand.

Weiss, meanwhile, hustled down the street in his postman's uniform, the duplicate package tucked jauntily under his arm, wondering to himself as he walked whether the fake mustache might not be a little too much. *Why is it that Dixon always looks good no matter how ridiculous the costume, and I always look ridiculous even when the costume's good?*

Sydney and Weiss approached Keiko from opposite directions, confident that by closing in on her they could salvage the drop and make the switch unnoticed, even if they were being watched. But just as they came in sight of each other, an exasperated driver laid on his horn, and Keiko seemed to emerge from her stupor. Her face brightened, and she turned on her heel and headed straight for the mailbox a block away.

"Looks like plan B is still in effect!" Sydney exclaimed into her comm.

"Then we'll make the switch at the mailbox as planned."

"Copy that."

Both agents slowed their pace, Sydney going so far as to lean gratefully on a telephone pole, feigning punk-attitude indifference but actually very glad to reduce the pressure on her still-weak leg. She twirled the cane and plastered a little *Clockwork Orange* snarl on her face as they watched Keiko stride up to the mailbox, open the slot, and thrust the package inside. Weiss approached, ready to hand off the replacement package.

But Keiko was trying to thrust the package in again. And again.

"It doesn't fit in the slot, Sydney," she whispered under her breath, not sure what to do.

Sydney rubbed her temple wearily. *If I'm going to have a career as a handler,* she thought, *I'm going to have to ask Vaughn for some tips.* "Look, Eric, we're just going to have to smash-and-grab this. Remember that op in Panama City?"

"If I remember right, Syd, that op involved me winding up flat on my back in the street."

"It could be worse. You could be in the street-urchin role and nursing a broken leg."

Weiss took a deep breath. "Fair enough. I'm ready when you are."

"Okay. Signal me when you're in position."

Weiss strolled up to a confused Keiko and, mimicking a mailman-on-the-go, began to fuss for a key to open up the mailbox. Keiko glanced at him, thinking she recognized him as Weiss, but she was thrown slightly by his mustache and his breezy "Top o' the mornin' to you!" She smiled stiffly in response, unsure what was expected of her.

"Outta the way!" Keiko turned to see a street punk, swinging a cane and boasting long, stringy blond hair, copious amounts of mascara, and a black zippered jacket, bearing down on them at top speed as she raced down the street. In the instant's time it took for her and the postman to topple to the ground, Keiko felt fleetingly sure that the punk who'd bumped into them was Sydney, and until the pain of hitting the pavement obliterated the thought, she found herself marveling at the cool costumes Sydney and her friends always seemed to be wearing. But then Keiko and Weiss were on the ground, bruised and groaning, their two identical brown-wrapped packages scattered around them. Sydney, chewing gum indifferently, looked down at them like she was annoyed they'd been in her way.

"Y'oughta watch where yer goin'," she spat.

"Seems to me, missy, that you were the one going. Which makes you the one who should be watching out," Weiss complained as he picked himself painfully up off the ground.

"'sa public thoroughfare," Sydney responded in a snotty tone, followed by a barrage of contemptuous chews.

"Do you think I don't know a sidewalk from a street, miss?"

"I think ya should shut yer mouth and let a girl get where she's going!"

Keiko got it: The escalating argument was meant to provide cover while she picked out the fake package, which she could then pretend was the one she'd been carrying all along. No one would notice. It was a perfect dead-drop. *Except I wish I hadn't had to get dropped myself,* she thought, rubbing her side tenderly.

That was when a screech of tires signaled the approach of a blue sports car, tearing around the bend and skidding to a stop directly beside them, leaving black marks on the road behind each tire. Sydney and Weiss tensed instinctively, but Keiko, drained of all the color in her face, seemed to go completely cold. The two agents exchanged worried looks as the car's passenger door sprang open. Keiko leaned down and looked in to see Franklin, glaring across the front seat and issuing a stark command. His voice made it clear that he wouldn't be taking no for an answer.

"Get in!"

CHAPTER 13

MOMENTS LATER
LOS ANGELES

Keiko had immediately done what her husband told her to do. She wasn't even aware of what she was doing. Frankin had said, "Get in," so she had gotten in. It was like someone else had done it, like some other person had elbowed her aside and took over, like she was reduced to watching helplessly as Keiko, whoever that was, meekly hopped into the car.

Franklin was smiling at her with that false, beneficent grin of his, so sure Keiko would go where he said, do what he wanted, and be the obedient, docile shell of herself that he seemed to want her to be. He repulsed her, and yet if she just stepped aside, or even let herself be pushed away, the other girl, pliant little Keiko, could stay with him and be happy, or something like it. What was happiness, after all, if it wasn't living blindly and peacefully, completely dazed, with a husband who transcribed her conversations with a father she could no longer get on the phone, whose voice felt cold on her skin, who loved her so much he hit her? All she would have to do was go away, or just keep quiet until finally she faded away. *That would be so easy. . . .*

"Keiko, darling!" Franklin said. "I didn't mean to startle you. I was just driving through town, and I remembered you had errands here this morning, and I thought I'd see if I could catch you on your way back. What lucky timing."

Keiko mustered a smile. It was slow coming, but most everything she did when he was around had a kind of sedated sluggishness to it, so he was probably used to it by now.

"What a pleasure to see you," he said. "You'd think that long, wonderful walk yesterday would have satisfied my hunger for your presence." He planted a kiss on her cheek. A second later, Keiko wiped her face when he wasn't looking. "Have I caught you before you had a chance to pick up that package? I didn't mean to interrupt the business of the morning. You did pick it up, didn't you?"

"I dropped it. . . . Just now. . . ." She gestured at Sydney and Weiss, still standing outside the open car door, looking in with expressions of total bafflement. They were each holding one of the packages. Keiko had lost track of which one was the real one and which one was fake. *That's true of myself, too,* she thought sadly. *I'm not sure which me is the real one anymore either.*

"Oh, well, that's no problem." Franklin rolled down the passenger-side window. "Excuse me out there! My wife's a bit clumsy sometimes, but it's so nice of you to pick that up for her." He looked at the two identical packages quizzically for a second. "I'm sorry, but one of those should be addressed to my wife, Keiko Thornhill."

"That'd be this one, sir," Weiss said, handing Franklin one of the packages. "We had a little spill out here—occupational hazard—but that one's the lady's." Franklin gazed at Weiss curiously. He was trying to place a vaguely familiar face, and Keiko was sure the arm in a sling was ringing a bell, but fortunately the exterminator from yesterday had made as little impression on Franklin as his wife's hard work around the house generally did.

"I appreciate it," Franklin said, eyeing the package greedily as he reached for it. "But is that . . . wait, is that Sydney Bristow?"

Sydney hesitated for a second, deciding how best to play this. "Yes, Franklin. I happened to meet Keiko at the post office and was walking back with her. It's nice to see you again."

"It's a little early in the day for a costume party," Franklin said, eyeing her skeptically.

"Actually, the party was last night. It went late. I'm on my way home now to crash. You know me, right? Up all night yet again!" She twirled her hair carelessly, playing the part of a party-girl to a T. She even snapped her gum a little, no longer the punk, now the wild child. *How'd she get so good at slipping into different roles, always keeping it together?* Keiko wondered. *I seemed to split apart just shifting from grad student to housewife.*

Franklin frowned disapprovingly but hopped out peremptorily and leaned the seat forward, beckoning Sydney inside. "Let us at least give you a ride. You're still recovering from that broken leg, aren't you? You shouldn't be walking on it."

"Well, I was on my way to your place, actually, to get that book from you, K."

"Yeah," Keiko said meekly.

"Well, then, in you go. Here, let me . . ." Franklin took the other package from Sydney before she could stop him, and in glancing at it, saw that it was also addressed to Keiko. "What's this?"

He looked confused to the point of anger. Keiko knew she needed to say something. This one was up to her. "There were two packages at the post office, Franklin. So I was bringing them both, until we had that little run-in with the postman. I hope that's all right, dear. You did want both packages, right?"

"Oh? Two of them? Interesting . . ." Franklin took the other package as well, and Weiss gave a little salute before sallying off. Franklin didn't notice, since he was distracted by the two packages. "They only mentioned one," he mumbled under his breath, puzzled.

"I gotta tell you, Franklin, I'm very glad for the ride," Sydney said brightly as she jumped in the car. "I'm bushed, and I didn't feel like hoofing it."

Franklin looked up, and then looked right at

Keiko. She smiled. He smiled too, but something was wrong. Then his confusion seemed to dissolve, and he was putting the seat back upright and getting in and gunning the engine. He adjusted the rearview, glanced back at Sydney, and shook his head disapprovingly.

"Partying all night, Sydney!" he scolded. "Really, I'm beginning to worry you might be a bad influence on my wife."

Sydney, over the course of her career, had pretended to be a lot of people. She could replicate almost any accent, speaking numerous languages with effortless fluency, and she made elaborate costumes look like her everyday garb. Nepalese natives couldn't distinguish her Tibetan from their next-door neighbor's, and she could disappear into disguises as varied as a duchess or a dogcatcher with equal ease. She had once evaded capture by a crime syndicate by convincing its boss that she was his long-lost sister—an achievement made no less noteworthy by the fact that the criminal in question was so drunk at the time he could easily have mistaken a donkey for his own wife—and she had never, not even once, blown her cover with a misused idiom or a mispronounced word.

Such mastery of the art of concealment made Sydney especially attuned to the nature of a deception being performed in her presence, and she knew that what Keiko was doing was not slipping into a role, but hiding defensively behind a wall. She could tell that her friend's emotional turmoil was cutting her off from the husband she hated and feared. *That's understandable,* Sydney thought, *but unless we want to blow the whole thing open and just take Franklin into custody, I need you in the game right now.*

"K hasn't told me a lot about what you do for a living, Franklin," Sydney said offhandedly, trying to relieve the tension in the car as Franklin pulled onto the Thornhills' street.

"And I don't know much about you, either," Franklin replied. "Which is all well and good, isn't it? How sad to think we must be defined by the dull work we do all day."

"I don't know about that," Sydney said, her eyes locked on Keiko's blank expression. "I like to think the skills I've acquired at the bank shape my personal life in all sorts of positive ways." Did she imagine it, or did Keiko twitch a little as she heard this? Was it the word "bank" that shook her?

"Fair enough," Franklin said, pulling into his driveway. He shifted the car into park and turned around to gaze at Sydney in the backseat. "But what we do is not who we are. Who we are depends on friends and family, the people who love us and the people we love. I like to think of myself as Keiko's adoring husband first and foremost, and a diligent scientist only insofar as it makes me a better spouse." He smiled creepily, then exited the car and tilted the seat forward to allow Sydney room to exit. Once she'd done so, he crossed and opened Keiko's door, waiting as she slowly stepped out.

"Thank you, Franklin," Keiko said limply.

"Come in, Sydney, come in. I'm grateful to anyone who promises to rid my house of one of Keiko's cursed books. The damn things are everywhere, and in no particular order."

"Glad to be of service," Sydney muttered softly, moving toward the front door and subtly glancing at the van pulling up to the curb a few houses down. *Eric,* she thought, *I sure hope that's you.*

"It's me, Syd," Weiss assured her without audible prompting. "And I gotta tell you, fake moustache burn is as horrible an on-the-job injury as getting shot." He rubbed his sore upper lip and cast an unpleasant sneer at the moustache in question, lying on the dashboard where he'd tossed it after ripping it off. *I swear*, he mused quietly to himself, *if I wasn't off the clock on this little operation, I'd be putting in for danger pay.*

Of course Sydney couldn't respond, though he thought he could hear her exhaling a sigh of relief as she strolled into the Thornhills' house. He also heard her speak to Keiko as she entered the living room. "Keiko, you sure keep a tidy—" The rest of her small talk was obscured by an earsplitting roar of feedback.

"Whoa, whoa!" Weiss shouted into the mike as he fruitlessly flipped switches in an effort to quiet the noise. "Syd, you have to turn off your comm! The bugs are already in place in the house, and you need to turn your earpiece off." He lowered the volume on one bug after another, but the feedback didn't go away. "Syd, we can't . . ."

He trailed off as he realized that the input levels from Sydney's earpiece had already gone to zero. She had turned it off. But the feedback was still there. Hunched in the back of the dark, cramped van, brows furrowed in thought, Weiss pondered what could possibly be creating all of the feedback until, with a resigned purse of the lips, he understood what was going on.

Sydney's wasn't the only earpiece in the house. *Which means,* Weiss realized, *that other people are listening too.*

Sydney excused herself to the bathroom for a second to turn off her earpiece. She wished she'd been able to leave it on—just in case—but it was comforting to think that Weiss was in the van listening through the bugs he'd installed yesterday. *All I need to do is give a shout,* she thought, *and the cavalry will come rushing in. Hopefully that won't be necessary.*

She sighed, steeling herself, and flushed the toilet for a little sonic camouflage. Then she stepped out of the small powder room and back into the powder keg.

"You could have damaged the contents quite severely," Franklin was hissing at his wife, brandishing the two packages accusingly. "I ask you to pick something up, a simple job any idiot could have handled. You can't do a single thing right—"

"Uh, thanks for letting me, um . . . ," Sydney said, walking into the room. She saw Keiko cowering in a corner as Franklin berated her, but he turned around and regarded Sydney warmly as she reentered.

"Of course," Franklin said graciously. "Any time."

"Sydney's had a couple of really big deals go through at the bank recently," Keiko piped up abruptly. Both Franklin and Sydney looked at her in surprise.

"Is that so?" Franklin asked, his eyes returning to the packages. He clearly wished he could get his guest out the door so he could rip the boxes open in private, but he had to keep up with the conversation in order to allay any suspicions. His eyes snapped back to Sydney, and he feigned interest in her career advancement with considerable skill. "You know, even though I don't like talking shop, I am fascinated to know how you keep up with your work despite staying out all night on a Sunday."

Sydney was fixated on the packages as well, but for her purposes the best course of action was to keep the conversation going and thereby distract Franklin from them. "I'm sure you, as a scientist, know what I mean when I say that inspiration doesn't always occur on schedule," she said nonchalantly, dropping into a seat on the sofa and examining her fingernails. "Some investment opportunities are sealed on the dance floor, you know. Welcome to the twenty-first century." She hated the party girl/banker persona she'd fallen into, but right now she had no choice but to play it up.

"Tell me about it," Franklin said. "I swear some nights the test tubes only come alive at the witching hour."

"Perhaps I should get us some drinks," Keiko suggested in a flat, dead tone. "Some iced tea, maybe?"

Franklin and Sydney nodded, and Keiko stepped into the kitchen. Sydney rose and pretended to inspect the bookcases for the volume she was supposedly here to pick up. *Franklin was telling the truth about one thing,* she mused. *Keiko definitely does have more than her share of books.* The bookcases were so thickly stocked that there was a second row of books behind the first, with more stacked haphazardly on top.

"You don't know what a struggle it was just to convince her to try to put them all in one place," Franklin said. "And they still spilled over into my office. It's funny, because I never catch her reading them."

"Perhaps she reads when you're not watching," Sydney said idly.

"Some sort of covert reading operation, you're suggesting?"

"Even married people sometimes have secrets from each other." Sydney paused, her eyes leaving the table of contents of a dull-looking monograph on the Lost Generation to flit toward Franklin. He stood staring at her, one eyebrow raised in either suspicion or mock shock.

"If I were to find out that my wife was reading books on the sly," Franklin began, his tone full of what might be facetiousness, "my, what a rage I'd fly into!"

Sydney managed a forced smile but let the conversation drop. Turning back to the bookshelf, curious to see what had been relegated to the rear row, she moved aside a stack of paperbacks and found, much to her surprise, a set of first-edition Faulkner titles that she remembered Keiko had been overjoyed to find in a New Orleans bookshop six years ago. Absently, Sydney ran her finger over the spine of *As I Lay Dying,* then brushed away a layer of dust that had collected on her fingertip. Franklin saw her rubbing the dust and snorted.

"The woman's a miserable cleaner. She hasn't dusted in weeks. I promise to scold her soundly for that grime, Sydney."

Sydney didn't even bother to fake a smile. Instead, her hand curled into a fist behind her back.

It is not an easy thing to brew a superb glass of iced tea. Keiko was a bit fussy about it, having acquired an appreciation for the finer points of leaves and tannins from a father who delighted in the tea ceremony and obsessed over the perfect pot of darjeeling or Lapsang souchong. Iced tea, of course, was an abomination in his eyes; the perfect temperature for serving tea, Hikaru Terajima would always insist, varied from brew to brew, but was never below seventy-two degrees centigrade. Keiko, however, had grown to love the distinctly American, and oddly housewifely, task of seeing to it that tea was steeped for the perfect length of time prior to chilling, or that the precise amount of sugar was laced through the tea's flavor. Indeed, in her more meditative moments, it occurred to her that her entire life of late had been devoted to the task of masking the bitter with the sweet. She had grown quite skilled at it.

Her father would likely approve of her appreciation for the drink, having so many times extolled the curative powers of tea and the centering sense of peace that he claimed the tea ceremony offered him. *I wish you were here, Daddy,* she thought as she swung open the refrigerator and reached for the ornate glass pitcher on the top shelf.

She was coming back to herself, slowly but surely. The heft of the full pitcher in her hand as she lifted it from the shelf was comfortingly real, and the chill of the refrigerator door handle was distinctly close, not faraway and detached the way things had been in the car. Keiko even took a moment to hold the pitcher to her nose and inhale deeply, relishing the fresh odor of the mint she'd added to the tea. *Things are going to be okay,* she told herself.

In fact, Keiko would never pour a glass of iced tea from that pitcher. When she swung the refrigerator door shut, she found herself face-to-face with a very large man, dressed all in black, standing behind it. Down went the pitcher, open went her mouth, and off went the impulse from her brain to her larynx to initiate a very loud and very terrified scream.

Is she serious?

"Really? *Intruder in the Dust*? That's the book you came to borrow?"

"No one has a more complete Faulkner collection than Keiko, Franklin. And I've been meaning to read that one for a while now."

Well, let it not be said that the girl lacks a sense of style in her lying! Referencing the dust on the shelves and her own status as an interloper in my home, eh? Quite clever, quite clever. Me, I'm not sure what I'd have said in her position, if I was asked to name the book I was pretending to want to borrow. Probably I'd have made up a title, something realistic sounding but obscure, so that I'd have an excuse to look through all the shelves for a very long time before finally proclaiming the book nowhere to be found. That's assuming, I suppose, that she's here to snoop around the place. Is it possible she has a different agenda?

"I believe, Sydney, that that particular title is among the volumes relegated to my office."

"Oh, well then . . ."

"No, no. I'll get it. You set yourself down here and rest that leg of yours. I'm sure that in mere moments Keiko will be back with a . . ."

What just happened? She seemed so focused on those packages, not even hiding her disappointment when I picked them up to carry them into the office with me, and then all of a sudden she sat bolt upright, like . . . well, like someone was suddenly whispering in her ear! Is it possible that her target in entering my home is the packages? And is she on comms with backup agents who could enter at any moment? Gracious, I may not have much time. I've got to decide on a course of action. But decisions depend on information, and as yet I don't even know what the variables are. Need to retreat, ponder, assess.

I'll fake one last smile as I step away toward my office: "Anyway, as I say, Sydney, make yourself at home." *Cap it with a little bow. Except she doesn't notice: She's looking back toward the kitchen. Suddenly distracted, eh? Should I be concerned about this? No, let's deal with one thing at a time. Quickly: I need to make my way to the office and find out what's going on with these packages.*

Good, now the door's shut, I'll just put a chair

in front of the knob to secure it, take a seat, and have a look-see. This first one: From its weight, I know what this is. I was expecting it. But what's the second one? What else would they send, wrapped so similarly, shaped so . . .

What?

What is this? Why would they send this?

Is this some sort of . . .

Wait. Wait. The postman: He looked oddly familiar, didn't he? And Sydney happened to be there with a second package, this package, made up to look the same. Could the "postman" have been stationed outside the post office, ready to manufacture a duplicate? That's how I'd have run it, if I were in their position. They must have made this one, and they were going to switch them, and I interrupted. Which is why she's returned here, because the mission to retrieve the package is incomplete. How far will she go to complete it? What do I need to do to stop her? What are the knowns, and what are the unknowns?

The primary unknown is the identity of the person talking to her through an earpiece. But there definitely is someone, which means one known is that this place is almost certainly bugged. Which means she knows I've opened this second package and discovered this, this . . . fabrication. That's unfortunate.

Well then. Only one thing to do.

Let's see: Where did I put it? Oh, yes. In the compartment hidden on the bottom of the golf trophy. The latch is somewhere around . . . ah, yes. Right there. Good. Yes, yes. It feels good to hold this in my hand, to feel it so weighty and so fierce. It feels like safety.

Now . . . where did I hide those bullets?

"Syd, can you hear me?"

Sydney jumped despite herself. The last thing she expected was to hear a voice in her ear, since she'd turned off her earpiece. The surprise had to be obvious on her face, and Franklin must have noticed it. He trailed off, looking suspicious, but he collected himself swiftly.

As Franklin strode out of the living room toward his office, Sydney scanned the room for any more potential surprises. She was pleased to discover that once Franklin had gone, the living room was empty of anything suspicious.

"Michael?" she whispered. "Is that you? What's going on?"

"It's me, Syd. Are you alone?"

"For the moment, yes."

"It's a good thing that earpiece activation override code worked," Vaughn said, audibly relieved. "Look, there's no time to explain. You just need to get Keiko and get out of there."

"Why? And how did you know I was here?" Sydney rose and returned to the bookcase. She looked beyond the titles on the spines and noticed tiny wires running behind the rows of books. *This whole house is wired for sound,* Sydney realized. *But are there other bugs besides mine and Weiss's and Vaughn's?*

"Short version: Franklin's name set off alarm bells, Jack tasked me to watch you, and from where I'm sitting it's obvious that you're about to have visitors. And suffice it to say they don't look like nice guys."

"Keiko?" Sydney called out tensely into the kitchen. "Keiko? Are you okay?"

As if in response, Sydney heard the distinctive sound of smashing glass, and Keiko emerged from the kitchen clutching the handle of what used to be a pitcher.

"Sydney! There's a man in the—"

"I know, K." Sydney clutched her cane and placed herself between Keiko and the kitchen, ready to defend her friend. "Stand back."

"Yes, darling," came an unpleasant voice from behind them. "Please do stand back."

The two girls spun around to see Franklin stepping into the room, leveling a pistol at them menacingly and looking more than ready to use it.

"Michael, I could use some help," Sydney intoned, pressing a finger to her ear with the hand that wasn't gripping the cane like a quarterstaff.

"Two minutes out," the voice in her ear replied.

It was a lucky break for Keiko that her attacker had only two hands and astonishingly quick reflexes. One gloved hand sprang into action and covered Keiko's mouth, muffling her scream. The other reached down and palmed the falling pitcher so it wouldn't hit the ground and make a noise that might arouse suspicion. Suffice it to say, the entire maneuver was a pretty fine feat of coordination, but it left the man with both hands in use, leaving him with no means to stop Keiko from grabbing hold of the pitcher's handle and swinging it up and into his face. Limp sprigs of mint clung wetly to his face as he fell to the floor where glass shards glittered amid puddles of tea.

"Keiko? Keiko, are you okay?"

Still holding the pitcher's handle, Keiko raced out into the living room, exchanging a few words with Sydney about the man in the kitchen before Franklin appeared, brandishing a gun.

"Michael, I could use some help," Sydney had intoned mysteriously.

I could've sworn the guy's name was Eric, Keiko thought, right before gritting her teeth and lunging at Franklin. She swung the jagged-edged pitcher handle at him savagely. A grunt escaped her lips as she put every ounce of her strength into the blow, but Franklin sidestepped the swing. The handle wound up hitting the wall behind him and embedding itself in drywall. Keiko regarded him fearfully while shaking the hurt of the impact from her wrist.

"What are you doing? This is no place for you," Franklin snapped at Keiko, shoving his wife aside so she stumbled and fell. When Keiko looked up from where she lay sprawled on the floor, she saw that Sydney was swinging her cane fiercely, knocking the pistol out of Franklin's grip.

Keiko had some experience with being knocked down by Franklin, so it didn't shock her as much as it might have had this been their first physical altercation. She did a quick check to see if she'd broken anything, but other than a spot on her leg that would soon be black-and-blue, she was unhurt. Sydney, by contrast, was limping severely, but somehow still managed to look spry. With only occasional grimaces of pain, she ducked punches from Franklin and landed several blows, tripping him up with a swirling, low spin using the cane that looked a little like she was batting in a baseball game against a team of ants.

Franklin fell heavily to the floor not far from Keiko, who leaped up in fear. Sydney took advantage of Franklin's prone position to make a lunge for the gun.

"Take cover, K!" she gasped as a well-placed kick from Franklin hit her in the stomach.

"Don't forget the man in the kitchen!" Keiko cried out before scrambling down the hallway, bent on finding a weapon of some sort that she could use to help Sydney subdue her husband. She could hear the fight continuing in the living room as she made her way into Franklin's office.

She breathlessly started searching. Her eyes scanned over the jar of pencils, a paperweight, a golf trophy. *The trophy has possibilities, since it's nice and heavy. Wait, what's this stuff on Franklin's desk? A copy of* Houdini: His Legend and His Magic *by Doug Henning, half-wrapped in brown paper? That must be the fake package. Which means the real package is in here somewhere.*

Keiko rustled through the brown paper on Franklin's desk until she found the real package, which she tore open frantically, listening to the thuds of Sydney and Franklin throwing each other against the wall that separated the office from the living room. Inside the package was a compact metal case secured with a complicated combination lock. *Time to see what everyone's making such a fuss about,* Keiko thought. But the lock wouldn't open, and repeated bashings with the paperweight only produced a long spiderweb crack in the paperweight itself. *Why couldn't this thing have a weak lock like that stupid drawer?*

Just then a loud, dull noise sounded, and Keiko looked up to see the tip of Sydney's cane poking into the office through the drywall. Sydney must have lunged at Franklin and missed. As the cane disappeared back into the living room, an idea occurred to Keiko.

"Sydney!" she cried. "Sydney! Can you hear me?"

She received no answer.

"Oh, wait!" Keiko exclaimed, a lightbulb going on in her head. "Um, Eric? Or Michael? Whoever's listening to the bugs in this room, could you tell Sydney to do that thing with her cane again, only this time do it, like, six inches to the right?"

Keiko wasn't entirely sure this would work, but she pressed the metal case to the wall half a foot to the right of the hole and waited tensely for a moment or two before another loud, dull noise signaled a second wall-penetrating blow with the cane. Unfortunately, the new hole appeared about a foot to the left of where Keiko was holding the case.

"Oh! Sorry. I meant my right. Her left. Can you tell her that? Sorry about the mix-up. I'm new at this."

Silence answered her once again, and a moment later there was another sharp noise, this time from behind the case, and Keiko felt the metal shell give way. The cane's tip had thrust through the wall and directly into the case, the force jarring the lock and breaking it open. Keiko shut her eyes tight as the case broke apart in her hands, not sure what to expect. A small metal object fell to the floor at her feet.

"Thank you!" Keiko shouted as she knelt down to examine the contents of the case. "And, uh, if this is Michael Vaughn, Sydney's boyfriend, I, um . . . I really look forward to meeting you sometime. You sound very sweet."

She was surprised to find that the object was a cell phone. It looked familiar, but she couldn't quite place it. After looking at it for a second she noticed a note tucked inside the broken case. It read:

> F—Waiting for you to make progress with K has exasperated us to the last degree. If her resistance to your methods of persuasion continues, we will have to send someone to ask more forcefully. Your last chance with her is enclosed. We believe this phone contains HT's notes on the new rocket engines, but it is password protected, and he continues to refuse to talk. Make K reveal his password, or you will both face the consequences.

Suddenly Keiko realized where she'd seen this phone before: *It's my father's!*

* * *

Dixon emerged groggily from unconsciousness. He heard Vaughn's voice faintly in the distance.

"Sydney, Keiko wants you to puncture the wall with the cane again, only six inches to the right."

Dixon turned toward the voice, coming to slowly, and saw Vaughn climbing in through the kitchen window. Vaughn's face registered surprise at the sight of Dixon. Dixon guessed this was because his face was covered in soggy mint leaves. Vaughn pressed his finger back to his ear.

"Oh, wait, Syd. She meant her right, your left. Can you do it again? Thanks." Then he turned to Dixon. "You okay?"

A loud bang could be heard from the next room. Dixon wiped the mint off his face, brushed himself off, and looked at the shattered glass all around him on the floor. "I tried to tell her we were on her side, but she was too quick," he muttered in amazement as Vaughn helped him up.

"Former grad students," Vaughn sympathized. "They're tougher than you'd expect. I speak from experience." Dixon smiled. "Feel up to a little fighting?" Vaughn asked, glancing over his shoulder toward the living room.

Dixon nodded gamely, and the two men burst into the living room just as Keiko rushed in from the office.

"Sydney, they've got my father!" Keiko exclaimed, brandishing the cell phone angrily.

The three of them stopped short when they saw that Franklin had gotten his hands on either end of Sydney's cane and was using it to hold her in place, choking her with the wood. Already infuriated that her husband was attacking her friend, Keiko registered shock at the sight of two men, one of whom she'd decked moments earlier in the kitchen, apparently coming to Franklin's aid. The two men rushed toward Franklin, obviously intent on helping him subdue Sydney.

I'm not strong enough to stop three men, Keiko thought grimly. *I'm going to have to get help.*

Decisively, Keiko raced out the front door, grabbing Franklin's keys from the side table as she went, leaving Sydney to temporarily fend for herself. She felt a twinge of guilt, but she'd seen Sydney in action and felt confident that she could manage on her own until Keiko returned. She raced to Franklin's sports car and hopped in.

I'll be back, Syd. I promise. With practiced

skill, she turned the key and gripped the gearshift, gritting her teeth with determination. She punched the clutch and sped out of the driveway, shifting into gear and tearing off down the street. In her rearview, she could see the two men running out of the house after her, but she knew she was in no danger. She could outdrive them easily.

It's lucky Sydney taught me to drive stick all those years ago, Keiko mused as she sped away.

Waking up in the darkness, Weiss remembered only dimly the events that had taken place prior to his losing consciousness. He'd seen Vaughn emerge from the Mosquito Bandito van and sneak into the kitchen window, and he'd realized that the other bugs must be APO issue. *Vaughn's been spying on our op!* he'd suddenly understood, and he'd decided to take up a surveillance position closer to the house, in case backup was needed.

Creeping along the side of the house, he'd seen Keiko run out, hop into a sports car, and race away. Vaughn and Dixon had emerged from the house after her, shouting, but she'd been long gone, moving way too fast to hear them. *That girl sure knows how to drive,* he'd marveled, watching her disappear in a cloud of dust. Weiss had been about to step out and greet his friends—he'd even been looking forward to the looks of surprise they'd probably have on their faces when they realized how many APO agents were in on this—when his eyes had locked on something across the street, just beyond Vaughn and Dixon in his line of vision: A Roach-B-Gone Exterminators van.

He and Syd and had come in the Anti-Ant van, repainted brown. Vaughn and Dixon must have been in the Mosquito Bandito van. Which meant someone else was in the Roach-B-Gone van. *But who?*

An answer of sorts had come in the form of a blunt object connecting heavily with the back of his skull, and he'd fallen to the ground before Vaughn and Dixon had even had a chance to realize he was there.

Who knows how long I've been out, or where they've brought me, Weiss thought, struggling to his feet and fumbling around in the darkness. Wherever he was, it smelled foul, and he could hear a faint buzzing sound in the distance. Inside he could only feel the metal of some sort of machinery, and some enormous canisters of an undetermined liquid. By touch, he felt out one wall of the immense room he was in, and followed it until he found a door. It was unlocked.

Blinding light greeted Weiss when he swung the door open and stepped outside. He jogged about twenty yards out, anxious to escape the dank room where he'd been laying unconscious. As his eyes adjusted, he detected the swirl of dry wind all around him, and the ever-louder buzzing sound seemed to grow closer by the moment. Eventually his vision cleared, and he saw that he'd just emerged from a huge factory in the middle of a vast desert.

Where the hell am I?

But it wasn't his geographical location that was of immediate concern. It was the fact that he was in the direct line of flight of a crop duster, which had been buzzing through the sky overhead and was now hurtling lower and lower, aiming its front propeller directly at him. He turned and fled, running as fast as he could through the loose sand and diving to the ground just in time to avoid being turned into propeller grist.

This seemed a lot more elegant when Cary Grant was doing it, Weiss thought as he struggled to his feet, preparing to flee once again as the crop duster circled around for another pass.

CHAPTER 14

LOS ANGELES
LATER

MARK BAKER read the plaque in large capital letters, with his title, JUNIOR AGENT, in smaller type below. The agent in question adjusted the nameplate carefully, lining it up with the blotter on his desktop, then deciding, after leaning back and contemplating it a bit, that it would sit better slightly to the left.

Mark was proud of his plaque. It had been a gift from his mother following his recent promotion, and he displayed it prominently on his desk, which might not exactly occupy prime APO real estate, but it was far better than the basement cubicle in a dingy office building where he'd spent much of his CIA apprenticeship. The path upward through the espionage ranks was a rocky one, Mark always told his mom, and assignment to Arvin Sloane's small but well-regarded Los Angeles operation was a major advancement. Sure, he was making a lot of coffee, but he fancied that some of his superiors—the mysterious Michael Vaughn, for instance, or the fun-loving Eric Weiss—truly liked him. And though he knew he didn't have much of a chance with APO's top female agents—tough-as-nails Sydney Bristow or friendly-but-taken Nadia Santos—Mark sometimes indulged the fantasy that under other circumstances, it might have worked out. He even felt like Jack Bristow was starting to hate him a little less, and as for Sloane, well, a guy like that was hard to read. All in all, Mark felt like this was a place where he belonged, like he was part of the APO family.

To be sure, he'd made a major ally in Marshall Flinkman, who had found in Mark a willing ear and at least a small measure of comprehension. Each breakthrough in the op-tech lab sent Marshall scurrying to Mark to give him a full play-by-play, and Mark usually understood maybe forty percent of what he heard. And the remaining sixty percent of the time, Mark displayed a remarkable ability to nod and murmur appreciatively, regardless of how little he actually got what Marshall was saying.

He was nodding and murmuring even now as Marshall sat in front of him and raved about an obscure chemical compound he'd just analyzed. Mark had responded affirmatively to Marshall's introductory "Hey, Mark, remember that antidote we got from Arnold Paulson?" Mark, in fact, did not remember it, but that was beside the point. He had gone on to produce a very interested-sounding "Oh, really?" when Marshall had expounded on how after reverse-engineering the poison that it counteracted, he'd determined that it neutralized one of the most toxic concoctions he'd ever seen in all his years of biochemical study. For good measure, Mark had even offered an "Oh, you're just being modest" when Marshall had gushed that Paulson's chemical technique was so skilled, it almost confounded even him. Marshall had liked this last bit and had conceded that he'd figured it out in the end, after all.

"But seriously," Marshall had continued, "you should see how this antidote operates! It neutralizes the poison almost immediately, even outside the body, matching each chemical receptor electron for electron. It's like when a demolition crew implodes a house by placing charges at each of the building's critical load-bearing points, until the house is, like, 'Whoa!' And down it goes. That's how this poison is counteracted. It's like, all unsuspecting, like it says, 'Hi. Mr. Antidote, what a pleasure to meet you.' And then it extends its hand in a, like, how-ya-doin' kind of, friendly kind of way, only to have the poison go WHAMO! It grabs its hand and completely judo flips it over until the poison's like, 'Please, don't hurt me!' That Paulson is one smart guy."

Through much of this speech, Mark was reconsidering the position of the plaque. "Yes, he sounds like it," he'd responded automatically when Marshall paused, and then he leaned forward to nudge the plaque back a little toward the center.

"Marshall?" Sloane's voice prompted Marshall to stand up swiftly—so swiftly, in fact, that he forgot that Mark's desk was in a cramped back corner of the APO offices where the ceiling sloped downward sharply, and he hit his head hard against it. He was rubbing the bump tenderly when Sloane appeared.

"Do you have the . . . What's going on here?"

"I'm fine, Mr. Sloane," Marshall responded, embarrassed but clearly in a considerable amount of pain.

"Good. Do you have that report on the poison yet? Langley is anxious to work up casualty projections."

"I'm about to write it up. Basically, what we've determined is that it's got about an eight- to fifteen-hour incubation period after dermal exposure, during which you grow feverish and probably lose clarity of thought, and then, well, things get ugly after that. You start shaking uncontrollably, and then it gets worse. I gotta say, I wouldn't want to come into contact with this stuff."

Sloane said nothing, but his eyes made it clear that Marshall should be writing this rather than saying it. Marshall got the message, nodded a farewell to Mark, muttered "Excuse me," and rushed off. Sloane remained where he was.

"Baker," he intoned, in what was just about the friendliest greeting he'd ever given the junior agent, "have you worked up a facial recognition match for that photo I sent in from London?"

"Top of the to-do list, sir," Mark answered brightly, resolving to actually put it at the top of his to-do list straightaway. He'd gotten a little frustrated when his initial stabs at the task had yielded a bunch of unrecognizable phrases that he assumed were gibberish.

Sloane's lip twitched, but he said nothing. Instead, he turned to another junior agent who had walked in behind him, a comely young thing named Tracy who, Mark knew, nursed ambitions within the organization that he feared might one day conflict with his own. Mark hid his sneer as, with an efficient smile, Tracy stepped up to hand Sloane a clipboard.

"Someone to see you, sir," Tracy said, giving Mark a taunting little I-know-something-you-don't-know smile. Mark rolled his eyes.

Sloane examined the clipboard, his eyebrow raising in interest. "Send her to my office," he said simply and strode away, with Tracy trotting briskly behind him. Neither acknowledged Mark before departing.

Mark didn't have long to dwell on his bitterness. His attention was soon drawn to a chaotic scene out in the main bullpen area. He stood up and peeked out from his dark little corner into the brightly lit APO central hub. *One day I'll have a desk out there, where the action is,* he thought enviously as he watched Sydney shuffle a handcuffed man through the entranceway. He imagined with some satisfaction how nice the plaque with his name would look when it said something more impressive than "junior agent" underneath.

"Mr. Dixon!" he called out before he could stop himself. "Uh, Marcus?"

Dixon was hurrying past his office, and Mark took the liberty of tagging along beside him.

"What is it, Baker?" Dixon asked peremptorily.

"Uh . . . How's it goin'?"

Dixon stopped. Mark stopped too. Dixon glared at him, tilting his head, deciding whether or not to scold Mark for interfering with the business at hand. Then he let out a little sigh and placed a hand on Mark's shoulder. "You probably noticed we have a man in for interrogation. Why don't you sit in and observe?"

"Really, sir?" Mark could barely contain his excitement. "That would be awesome."

Dixon grinned and tried not to look condescending. He'd been a junior agent once too, and he knew how it was. With a tilt of the head that signaled *follow me,* Dixon proceeded on through the bullpen toward one of the glass-walled conference rooms, where the cuffed man—a glance at a prisoner log-in sheet told Mark his name was Franklin Thornhill—

could be seen slouching in an uncomfortable chair.

Mark followed, a few steps behind, but he couldn't suppress his excitement. He celebrated by making a two-second detour over to the desk that Tracy was using, where he glanced around, decided he could get away with it, and delicately placed a thumbtack on the seat of her chair. With a malicious chuckle, he fell back in behind Dixon. *That'll take the smile off her face,* Mark thought gleefully.

"Chatter confirms it," Dixon announced as he walked into the conference room, Mark entering behind him. "Weiss has been kidnapped by Dark Cloud."

"Hi, Ms. Bristow," Mark offered shyly, raising his hand in a half wave. Sydney, leaning on the conference table lost in thought, didn't acknowledge him. She was made up in mascara and wearing a punk outfit that Mark thought suited her perfectly. Her blond wig had been removed and tossed on the table. Mark thought it probably looked good as a part of the disguise, although he felt she looked best with her natural hair color. He had a little bit of a crush on her. But then, who didn't? *I mean, look at her. . . . Focus, Mark,* he told himself. *This is a learning opportunity, so watch, listen, and learn.*

"What do you know about this, Franklin?" Sydney asked sharply.

"What could I possibly know?" Franklin said mockingly. "I'm just a lowly, following-in-my-father's-footsteps spy, like you."

"You missed that part, Marcus," Sydney explained to Dixon, clearly deeming Franklin to be lying. "Franklin claims to be the son of an ex-CIA assassin."

Dixon looked a little abashed. What he was about to say wasn't really something that should come up in an interrogation where everyone involved needed to appear completely in command of all pertinent information, but they hadn't had time to brief Sydney on the relevant intel. "Well, actually, Syd, he is. Franklin Thornhill happens to be—"

"Ooh, he's not the son of Roger Thornhill, is he?" Mark piped up excitedly, pleased to be able to show off a little knowledge. "What an amazing coincidence! Sydney, didn't your father kill his dad in New Orleans a few years back?" Dixon and Sydney turned to look at Mark incredulously. "I've, um, been reading through the old ops logs," Mark explained, turning crimson as he realized that he should keep his mouth shut. "Maybe I'll, uh, sit over here." He took his seat meekly in a corner, and Dixon and Sydney turned away from him, shaking their heads.

"The Bristows aren't the only family that spies together, Sydney," Franklin offered in a chilly tone. "When I learned that my father had been killed, I set out to do what I thought he would want me to do. I was determined to complete his final mission. But it proved difficult to accomplish, because as I was stalking the target and preparing to kill her I, um . . . I began to feel things for her. In short, I fell in love." For the first time since Sydney had met him, Franklin's cold veneer broke. A tear escaped his left eye and rolled pitifully down his cheek. "I found I couldn't possibly kill an angel like Keiko Terajima, and to protect her, to keep her close and fend off anyone else who might be hired to eliminate her, I married her."

"Keiko wasn't your father's target in New Orleans," Vaughn said accusingly. Everyone turned to see him standing in the doorway. He had entered unnoticed, holding a sheaf of papers. "Roger Thornhill was there to kill Sydney."

Franklin considered this for a moment. "I suppose I see how you might have made that assumption. The New Orleans job did indeed task my dad to assassinate a UCLA grad student who was in town for an academic conference, and if your intel was incomplete, your personal interest in Sydney might have led you to figure she was the target. But I assure you, my father was hired to kill Keiko."

"Why on earth would anyone want Keiko dead?" Sydney asked as Vaughn crossed the room and stood behind her, tossing the papers onto a desk and thrusting his hands in his pockets. Vaughn seemed oddly nervous, and kind of fidgety.

"Her murder was to be the first stage of an intimidation campaign directed at her father, Hikaru Terajima, whose gifts in rocket science are much coveted by the terrorist organizations that have evolved into the Dark Cloud sect. But why am I telling you this? If you've done your homework, you know this already."

"Humor us," said Vaughn flatly.

Franklin shrugged, then continued. "It was made clear to Hikaru, six years ago, that if he didn't cooperate, his daughter would die. He did not, but fortunately she didn't, either. Still, his knowledge remains the key to Dark Cloud's current plans, and they've been upping their efforts to break him down and force him to help them. The package that arrived this morning was proof that they've gone so far as to abduct him, and if I understand Agent Dixon's announcement about this Weiss character, then apparently your organization is getting close enough that they've begun abducting your people as well."

"You're lying," Sydney spat. "If Keiko was really marked six years ago, then why haven't there been subsequent attempts on her life?"

"There have been," Franklin said matter-of-factly. "I've foiled every one of them. I thought I was doing the same thing today when you people arrived. It seemed likely enough to me that frustration with her father would have led the Kim brothers to send assassins to our house, and I'd never seen either of you before." He looked at Dixon and Vaughn, then continued, "I even thought Sydney was an assassin, which was why I pulled that gun and tried to fight her off. I don't know much about her, as I said to her earlier."

"But you know my dad. You had photos of him in your desk."

"I researched my own father's death meticulously. I determined who killed him and I tracked down photos so that I would recognize him in case Jack Bristow ever came for me. The photos weren't easy to come by—"

"We can't believe anything this man says," Vaughn interrupted, to Sydney and Dixon's surprise. Franklin fell silent.

"I'm tempted to agree," Sydney noted. "You have a funny way of protecting Keiko, Franklin. One that predisposes me to assume you're a liar as well as a wife beater."

Dixon and Vaughn, who hadn't known about the physical abuse, recoiled in disgust. Franklin sneered.

"Love sometimes manifests itself in ugly forms," he said in a voice tinted with equal parts arrogance and self-loathing. "In my efforts to protect my wife, I took on a role as a double agent, pretending to be a member of a Dark Cloud subgroup that marries women so the sect can tighten the screws, so to speak, on their relatives. In order to preserve my cover within Dark Cloud, and to convince them to suspend their plans to kill Keiko, I've had to pose as a man who exerts absolute physical control over her. This has necessitated some unpleasant incidents, but emergency room bills are an excellent way to make my superiors believe that I'm keeping my wife in line. Everything I've done—everything—has been to protect her."

"Hitting her?" Sydney asked angrily, emotion overcoming her as she spoke. "Beating her? Breaking her arm?"

"I love my wife," Franklin seethed, a second tear rolling down his face.

Sydney lowered her head. Dixon and Vaughn were silent. The room seemed to have gotten very cold.

"How about a short break?" Dixon suggested. The other agents nodded in agreement.

"Maybe a little coffee," Sydney muttered.

Mark sat up briskly. "I'll get right on it!"

As he stood and exited the room, he overheard Sydney whispering to Vaughn, "Can I get a copy of whatever you know about this guy? Whatever it is you've been keeping from me?"

"Jack ordered a lid," Vaughn responded quietly. His tone was apologetic.

"Just . . . ," Sydney was holding back her anger in front of the other agents. "Can I just get the file?"

Vaughn frowned and nodded. He gathered up his papers and followed Mark out the door and down the hall to a computer terminal across from the coffee machine, where he and Mark threw themselves into their respective tasks. A lengthy silence, broken only by the clicking sound of Vaughn's fingers on the keyboard and the burblings of the coffeemaker, followed.

"Wow," Mark said finally, trying to start up a conversation. "Pretty intense in there, huh?"

"What's that?" Vaughn was clearly concentrating on printing out background information on Franklin. "Are you talking to me?"

Mark smiled. He loved this little game he and Vaughn played, where Vaughn pretended not to listen to things that Mark said. It was part of the close, almost brotherly relationship he was developing with the more experienced agent. *Brothers always give each other a hard time,* Mark thought with a little chuckle, *but there's a mutual respect here that no one can deny.*

"Yeah. No," Mark stammered. "I was just you know thinking that guy has a pretty twisted idea of love, don't you think?"

Vaughn turned, gave a very stiff nod of agreement, then seemed to fall into thought. His eyes were drawn to the sheaf of papers he'd been nervously fussing over in the conference room. "Have you ever done something you regret?" Vaughn asked suddenly. Mark was surprised by the personal question, and he pondered it carefully. Not getting an answer, Vaughn pressed on, though one might have thought he was talking more to himself than to Mark. "I mean, something you wish you hadn't done? Something where you'd give anything to be able to go back in time and undo it?"

"Um . . . do you mean not giving Ms. Bristow the files?"

"No," Vaughn snapped, suddenly seeming annoyed at Mark. "That was just following orders. I mean, something bigger. Something that could have really hurt somebody."

Realization hit Mark like a ton of bricks. *Oh, I get it.* He looked at the floor in shame. "Yeah, Agent Vaughn. I guess I have."

"Don't you wish you could have stopped yourself before it happened?"

Mark nodded. "Yes."

Vaughn seemed thoughtful for a moment, then stood up. He felt like he'd clearly reached an awkward place. He exhaled a long sigh. "Good talk, Baker," he said, then grabbed the printouts from the printer and hurried away.

"Uh, Mr. Vaughn? Michael?" Mark called out. But Vaughn had been too quick and was already out of earshot, which meant Mark couldn't tell him that he'd forgotten the original sheaf of papers he'd been carrying. Slyly, Mark flipped through them, but they weren't particularly interesting—just a collection of printed photos of Jack Bristow, apparently taken in a graveyard. *I've got bigger things to think about,* Mark decided. *I've just been reprimanded by my superior, who's also my good buddy. I've got to make things right while I still can.*

Deeply embarrassed, Mark methodically finished preparing the coffee with uncharacteristic solemnity. He placed the cups neatly on a tray and carried them back toward the conference room. Before he reached it, however, he stopped at Tracy's desk, set the tray down, and carefully removed the tack from her seat. *How'd he know? No wonder Vaughn's a top-ranked spy,* Mark thought. *But he's right. I'd have regretted doing this later on. It's good he stopped me before Tracy got hurt. That's what brothers are for: nudging you back on the right track.*

Pocketing the tack, Mark picked the tray back up and carried it into the conference room, where Dixon had resumed questioning Franklin as Sydney paged through the files Vaughn had brought her.

". . . and they want to seed the skies?" Dixon

was asking. "That's their plan? Surely they don't really think that can work. Trying to control the weather is like something out of a comic book."

"Cloud seeding has been a real-life tool of agriculturalists for decades," Franklin responded. "You basically nudge the preexisting moisture in the air into liquefying and forming droplets. It's not complicated. With Terajima's new rockets, however, this can be done on a grand scale, making it rain over an enormous area, and the rain can be seeded with chemicals present in the rocket's payload."

"Which means you can create poison rain," Vaughn deduced.

"Coffee's ready," Mark jumped in, earning scowls from Sydney, Vaughn, Dixon, even Franklin. "I brought cream and sugar, too," he said in a weaker tone of voice, then pointed at Franklin and tried, unsuccessfully, to sound menacing. "But none for you. You get it black, and a little lukewarm."

Dixon encouraged Mark to stand off to the side, out of the way of the action, which he did.

"So where's the rain going to fall?" Sydney asked, looking up from the files.

"From what I hear," Franklin said, "tests are

going on even as we speak in a small factory town in the Chinese desert. They're using crop dusters and targeting small areas until Terajima's rockets are ready, at which point they'll launch the rockets and take aim at a major metropolitan center."

"Specifically?" Sydney demanded.

Franklin paused a moment. "One thing to remember about East Asia: For complex historical reasons, the Japanese are by far the least popular kids on the block."

"What's the target, Franklin?" Dixon sounded like he would break Franklin in two if he didn't cough up the information.

"Tokyo."

Dixon, Vaughn, and Sydney exchanged anxious looks. "We have some calls to make," Sydney said. The two men nodded, and all three agents departed briskly.

"Uh, guys?" Mark called after them. "Your coffee's gonna get cold. . . ." He crossed his arms and drummed his hands on his biceps idly as Franklin eyed him with masked amusement. Mark tried to put on a threatening face.

"Do you have calls to make too?" Franklin asked with mocking brightness.

"As a matter of fact, I do," Mark replied haughtily.

"Your real estate broker, I assume? To tell him to sell your extensive properties in Tokyo?"

"We're going to stop you," Mark said with utter certainty. "Believe it or not, the good guys always win."

Franklin guffawed. Mark was a little unnerved by how hearty and undignified his laughter was. "Forgive me," Franklin sputtered. "It's just, you're a very funny little man. You think you're one of the good guys, don't you?"

"Yes. I'm an agent in the Central Intelligence Agency, working for the greatest country in the—"

"Right, right. God bless America and all that. Look, I don't want to disillusion you, but aren't you actually an employee of APO?"

"Which is a division of the CIA. Not that classified information like that is any of your business," Mark scoffed.

"Have you ever heard of an espionage outfit called SD-6? No longer in existence, but it burned rather brightly in its day."

"Of course I've heard of it."

"And who headed that organization?" Franklin prompted.

"I see where you're going with this, but Arvin Sloane is reformed."

"Have you heard the old saying 'Fool me once'?" Franklin asked. "Well, if you really think the man has changed, then, well . . . shame on you."

Doubt crept into Mark's mind for a moment, but he quickly shrugged it off. "Even if you were right," he said confidently, "I don't think you're on very high ground here, pal. You work for a bunch of guys who are planning to make poison rain fall on Tokyo."

"I am a double agent within Dark Cloud. That's true," Franklin answered with equal confidence. "But my true loyalties lie with a real division of the CIA, the legitimate equivalent of what APO claims to be. My boss, Arnold Paulson, tells his employees all about Sloane's trick of making employees believe they work for Langley, when in fact they only work for him. . . ."

Paulson? Hadn't Mark heard that name before?

". . . and everyone, both in the main Loge-21 headquarters in Las Vegas and in remote outposts like my Manhattan Beach home, is well aware of the dangers of rogue operations that brainwash agents into mistakenly working against the CIA. It's sad that you've fallen for Sloane's little trick."

Loge-21? That sounded familiar too. Mark brushed aside Franklin's speech and hurried out the door, running smack into Tracy as he went.

"Ouch!" he exclaimed, clutching his side.

"I'm sorry," Tracy said. "I didn't mean to bump into you."

Mark was almost crying, it hurt so much. "Yeah," he gasped. "Me too. Sorry."

"It's no big deal. Don't be such a wuss," Tracy muttered as she walked away, shaking her head as she went. Was that a little spring in Tracy's step? Mark could have sworn he detected a touch of excitement in her gait.

But the pain took precedence over thinking about that. Mark held himself together until she was out of sight, then reached into his pocket, where the impact with Tracy had driven the thumbtack through the fabric of his pants and into his skin. He pulled the tack out and massaged the spot. *Oh well*, he thought resignedly. *It serves me right.*

Remembering what he'd meant to do, Mark rushed back to his desk, ducking down to avoid the low ceiling. He rustled through some papers until he found the photo Sloane had sent him for facial recognition scanning. Clipped to it was the initial set of results that Mark had dismissed as gibberish, and when he ran his finger down the printout he found exactly what he was looking for.

> Possible loyalties of unidentified suspect: LOGE-21, an indeterminate rogue agency, base of ops unknown, with constantly shifting CIA-friendly or -unfriendly status. Further investigation into LOGE-21 is pending.

This line was embedded in the middle of pages and pages of similarly speculative results, and Mark had dismissed it. But now it seemed like crucial information. He clutched the printouts close to his chest and rushed back out into the bullpen, turning a corner and catching sight of Sydney standing at the end of the hall.

"Miss Bristow! Uh, Sydney?" he called out excitedly.

"Just a second, Mark," she said, turning slightly to hold up one finger signaling him to wait. As she turned, Mark saw that she was deep in conversation with Vaughn and Tracy. *Wait, what's going on here?*

"And he claims that this 'Loge-21' is a legit

division of the CIA, and APO is the rogue?" Sydney was asking.

"That's exactly what he claims," Tracy was saying. "I hope you don't mind my stepping in to interrogate him further after you left, but I think the information I gleaned from him was worth the breach of protocol."

"Certainly," Vaughn agreed. "We'll see to it you're commended for this, Tracy." Tracy brightened and offered him a grateful flutter of her eyelashes. She was clearly a bit sweet on Vaughn.

Mark felt his mouth fall open in astonishment. "You were eavesdropping just now?" he whispered accusingly at Tracy, low enough that Sydney and Vaughn couldn't hear. Tracy just smiled, a cocky little you-snooze-you-lose grin. Once again, Mark found himself thinking about how he kind of hated this girl.

Sydney and Vaughn both thanked Tracy warmly, then rushed off, forgetting all about Mark. Tracy followed them, pleased to be the hero. Mark stood rooted in place, stewing for a moment, then returned to his desk. Finally, he had a minor epiphany: *Two can play at that game, Tracy.*

He stood up and walked back to the conference

room, strolling nonchalantly and keeping an ear open. As he sauntered past, he could hear the discussion inside clearly.

". . . so you've never actually been to Langley?" Dixon was asking.

"No, I haven't," Franklin replied, uncertainty creeping into his voice. "But that doesn't mean—"

"Yes, it does," Sydney said. "That's exactly what it means. You can ask this man, who wrote the book on this stuff." Mark assumed she was referring to Sloane, who seemed to have joined the interrogation group since Mark had left.

"I'm very impressed with Arnold," Sloane could be heard saying. "Warning his employees against subterfuge like the one that fueled loyalties to SD-6 is the perfect way to throw suspicion off himself. And giving the poison to Dark Cloud and the antidote to us, thus guaranteeing he'd be partnered with the winning side, regardless of who comes out on top, was a fine move."

"A maneuver worthy of you," Dixon said with what obviously wasn't admiration.

"Yes," said Sloane with some pride. "Indeed it is."

"Wait, let me get this straight," Franklin began,

obviously on the verge of being convinced. Mark walked out of earshot before he could hear the rest of Franklin's statement, however, and he didn't want to draw attention to himself by walking past the doorway a second time. *Darn, I didn't learn anything useful there! Why does Tracy get all the luck?* Mark thought, dejected.

"Baker!" Dixon's voice pulled him out of his thoughts. Mark spun around to see Sydney and Vaughn leaving; and Dixon calling to him on his way out. "Mr. Sloane wants to speak with you," Dixon finished, then walked away.

Mark hurried into the conference room and found Franklin and Sloane alone. Franklin was rubbing his wrists where the handcuffs, recently removed, had chafed them. "Yes, Mr. Sloane?" Mark asked. "Arvin? I mean, uh . . . sir?"

"Mr. Thornhill's coffee is cold," Sloane said. "Get him a fresh cup. He and I have a lot to talk about."

"I could care less about the coffee," Franklin replied. "Just let my wife go."

Mark was confused by this comment, so he looked up from gathering the coffee mugs and followed Franklin's gaze. Through the glass walls of the conference room, Mark saw a gorgeous Japanese woman sitting patiently in Sloane's office. Mark's eyes lit up in interest.

"Ah, yes, the lovely Keiko," Sloane said. "I hope she'll forgive me for glowering at her while you were talking to the others earlier. I had to make you think I would hurt her if you didn't cooperate. I imagine you'd have been less forthcoming otherwise."

Franklin gave Sloane a defeated sneer, and Sloane began his questioning. "Now then, you say there will probably be more abductions of APO personnel?" he asked, crossing to shut the door behind Mark.

The door closed, and Mark, bearing the coffee tray, could hear no more. On his way back to the coffeemaker, though, he passed Tracy, who gave him a little shrug from where she was leaning intently over a computer monitor.

"Hey, what's up with the girl in Sloane's office?" Mark asked.

"Her?" Tracy looked nonplussed. "She was a walk-in. She showed up at the old Credit Dauphine offices, believe it or not, and then was shuttled over here. I have no idea who she is." Mark nodded. "You know," Tracy continued, just shy of apologetically, "I feel bad about what happened back there. But sometimes you have to grab opportunities when they come up. It's how you get ahead. I hope there are no hard feelings."

"Of course not." Mark smiled. Tracy smiled back, and Mark continued on his way.

He made a quick detour, however, to place another tack on Tracy's chair. *No wait*, he thought to himself. *It should be just a little to the right. Just an inch or two. Right . . . about . . . there. Perfect.*

He stood back, admiring his handiwork with a smile. But just as he picked the tray up to resume his coffee-fetching duties, phones all over the office began to ring. It was like a symphony of telephones, and it was unlikely to mean anything good.

"Bad news is coming in from Tokyo!" someone announced loudly as the APO offices went into crisis mode. "Tell Mr. Sloane this is urgent!"

Well, one thing's for sure, Mark thought to himself, hurrying on and carrying the tray with a kind of professional pride. *Whatever's happening, they're gonna need lots of coffee!*

CHAPTER 15

TOKYO
MOMENTS EARLIER

The Japanese word for "beer" is *biiru,* and Jack Bristow uttered it while holding up two fingers, the back of his hand facing the waitress according to custom. She promptly brought a pair of sizable, foamy drafts, setting one near Jack and the other on the opposite end of the small table.

"A friend will be joining me shortly," Jack said in impeccable Japanese, indicating the empty seat across from him. The waitress bowed politely and withdrew. Unaccustomed to being kept waiting, Jack checked his watch and contemplated the drink. He had no intention of consuming it, and had simply ordered it so he'd have something in front of him while Honda, as was his habit, downed a beer or two. Though he'd never met the man, Jack knew a lot about Honda, an unpleasant little leech of a fellow whose predilection for liquor and women may well have been his most notable qualities. Having gazed at Honda's dull eyes in countless photos while reviewing intel during the flight over, Jack thought he would probably recognize the man regardless of lighting or disguise. Yet he didn't see him anywhere in the bar. And it was now ten minutes past the designated meet time. Some men would begin to display signs of impatience in a situation like this, but Jack simply internalized his annoyance, as he did every emotion. A slight tightness in the set of his jaw was the only indication of his displeasure.

The Japanese have an odd fondness for these superficially classy hostess bars, he reflected. Businessmen sat at almost every table, unwinding as they bantered with beautiful women who, though no one admitted it openly, were paid by the bar to entertain the customers. Each patron bought his companion's cocktails, paying the price of two drinks for every one consumed. The women's glasses, by tacit arrangement with the bartender, were invariably filled with water. The men grew drunker and drunker as the women feigned increased intoxication. At the end of the night, some of the less principled ladies made a little extra money by going home with the gentlemen they'd entertained all evening, which made the entire establishment not much more than a glorified bordello with a half-decent selection of karaoke options. In the twenty minutes Jack had been sitting alone, customers had pantomimed Britney Spears songs, one patron and a hostess did a passable rendition of a duet from *Grease,* and an older woman—likely the bar's owner—had sung a moving version of a classic Japanese *enka* hit from the 1950s.

"Is this seat taken, sir?" a woman asked him.

"It will be," Jack replied tersely, looking up at the hostess who had approached him. "Not to be rude, miss, but I'm not here for conversation. I'm meeting someone."

The girl, clad in a slinky dress that looked fresh from the most fashionable floors of Tokyo's swankest department stores, sat down across from him anyway. Her waist-length black hair draped down, cradling her face before moving on to cradle curvier parts of her body, and she reached out to take Jack's hand sensuously. Perhaps because he knew that the sensuousness was not attraction, at least not in the nonprofessional sense, Jack found her touch a tad cold. Or perhaps it was something else that made this act of hand-holding feel so unromantic. Perhaps it was that the woman was . . .

"Nadia?" Jack asked. He leaned into the table, inspecting her face closely as he pretended to be taken with the girl just like any other businessman there for the company of women. Nadia smiled and leaned in as well, brushing the hair of her wig back slightly so he could see her face more clearly.

"Yes, Jack. I've got a message from Honda."

"Where is he? I haven't spotted him, and I've surveyed everyone in the room."

"I'm not actually sure. I'm getting messages conveyed through middlemen. My guess is he's in the back somewhere. He may be in another building entirely."

Jack frowned. He didn't like being toyed with, and his tolerance for this sort of cloak-and-dagger situation had already been maxed out by his phone call to Sloane earlier. "So the meet is off?"

"I don't think so," Nadia assured him. "But—and I'm embarrassed to be the bearer of a message like this—he thinks you ought to sing a song first. He suggests you drink up a bit and then plug number forty-seven into the karaoke machine."

Jack was silent for a moment. "You're kidding," he finally said.

"I thought *he* was kidding," Nadia said. "But . . ." She trailed off, shrugging helplessly.

Efforts to make Jack Bristow angry were usually successful in ways that the people making the effort did not expect. Those wishing to goad him into acting thoughtlessly or rashly never achieved their goal. Those whose objective was to wheedle him into raising his voice, or betraying closely guarded information along with his anger, invariably failed. And those who simply wanted to get a rise out of him often found that Jack, once roused, tended to act quickly, and severely, and ruthlessly. More than a few who had made Jack angry had wound up dead shortly thereafter, or at least hospitalized for the foreseeable future. Kiyoaki Honda was, in short, playing with fire.

In this case, however, Jack was feeling charitable. He rose from the table and glanced over at the karaoke machine. The swig of beer he gulped down might, to an ignorant observer, have seemed like an effort to steel his nerves, but in Jack's case its purpose was merely to loosen his natural stiffness ever so slightly.

"Give it your best," Nadia said, reverting to the role of encouraging hostess and employing the Japanese idiom customary when wishing a patron luck.

"You," Jack replied with a slight slur as he wiped his mouth with the back of his hand, "are about to see something that few have seen."

Jack's impression of a drunken businessman was dead-on. He swung his hands broadly, blustering his way through the tables boozily. "Lemme at that microphone!" he shouted with liquor-fueled confidence. "Enough of these amateurs! Let a real singer take a shot at it!"

The room fell silent as he grabbed the mike out of the hands of a meek young woman and put it to his lips. A deafening burst of feedback screamed out of the speakers and Jack beat on the mike relentlessly, sending booming thuds echoing through the bar. The ladies covered their ears, and the men shouted angrily, but Jack just repeated "Is this thing on? Is this thing on?" until a bar employee rushed up and offered Jack a new microphone. Jack took the new microphone out of the box and began to speak into it louder than was necessary.

"So I've come 'ere from America to show you guys how to sing!" he slurred in English, moving the mike from one hand to the other and flexing his fingers before wiping them on a handkerchief he pulled inconspicuously from his pocket.

Nadia, still seated at the table, took a sip of beer, and then put her hand over her eyes, faking embarrassment. Behind her hand, she was actually smiling a little, impressed at Jack's ability to throw himself into this character.

"I'll sing you anything! Anything!" Jack seemed to be taunting the uncomprehending audience. He tucked the handkerchief away, then faked a losing-his-footing stumble against the monitor that controlled the karaoke machine. "How's 'bout I just punch in a random number, and sing that, huh?" His fingers shot out at the touchscreen before him, and it seemed as if he really was hitting random numbers. Nadia, however, knew that he was putting in the number Honda had directed. "Okay!" he said, steeling himself. "This song is called 'Beauty After Rain,' and it's originally by, uh . . . by . . ." He squinted at the screen as if he couldn't pronounce the singer's name. "Ah, who cares? Now it's by me!"

Nadia wondered if Jack knew the song, a quavering little tune by an emotionally fragile, slightly built indie rocker who, Nadia had read recently in a magazine, was currently dating his third movie star this year. It didn't seem like the sort of thing likely to pop up on Jack's radar. *The only person less likely than Sydney's dad to be familiar with the playlists on MTV2,* Nadia thought with a little giggle, *is mine.* Still, the man occasionally evinced a surprising familiarity with pop culture, and Jack's performance was solid enough that you had to conclude he either had a dead-on ear for melody, or he had learned the song ahead of time. The strength of his voice, obscured slightly by his faux drunkenness, was undeniable as he built richly to what, in the voice of the original artist, was a rather thinly melodramatic conclusion:

I will stay with you come what may
Listening to the raindrops hit the pane

Through the thunderstorms and hurricanes
Waiting for the beauty after rain . . .

Nadia was impressed. *In an alternate universe, Jack Bristow could star on Broadway.* But in this one, he received only slow claps and bemused praise from giggly hostesses who continued to nurse some hope that this boozing buffoon would tip them liberally. Jack looked at the screen to be sure the song was over, bowed deeply, then strode back to the table where Nadia was still sitting. He did not swerve or stumble; the drunk routine had ended. He sat down, reached for a napkin, and wiped his hands thoroughly.

"I wasn't given any other instructions, Jack," Nadia said after a moment. "I'm not sure what happens now."

"What happens now," Jack said, "is we go home. The screen that fed me the lyrics had a personal message from Honda at the end of the song."

"Which was . . . ?"

"'Mr. Honda sends his regrets.'"

"Really? I don't understand."

"Our time has been wasted. It's a shame, because this meet was crucial." Jack paused, still wiping his hands, as if he was unable to get them clean. "There was something on that microphone handle," he muttered softly.

"Well, at least your performance was strong," Nadia offered, putting as bright a spin on the situation as she could muster.

"It's all in the song," Jack said distractedly. "That tune was completely overwrought. It was an absolute delight to sing. What a sense of humor the songwriter must have." His voice was utterly mirthless as he said this. Jack stood up abruptly. "How are you feeling, Nadia?"

Nadia was taken aback. "Um, fine."

"If you'll excuse me a moment, I think a hand washing might be in order."

Nadia seemed confused, but Jack had already departed, walking briskly toward the bar's restroom. His gaze was fixated on his hands, and his mind was working fast. *Something's wrong,* he mused. There was no reason Honda would have him sing that song and then terminate the meet. *They had me drink, and then they had me sing. Could they have drugged the beer? No, Nadia drank as well, and she's fine. Wait—isn't Paulson's poison transmitted through the skin? Could they have put the poison on the microphone handle?* Jack thought frantically.

By this time Jack was alone in the bar's restroom, scrubbing his hands but still feeling something odd coursing through his veins. *Another call to Arvin is in order,* he thought. *I need him to send me some of that antidote he says they're making.* He dried his hands, then reached into his pocket to fish out his cell phone. But he never got to make the call.

"Please remove your hand slowly from your jacket, Mr. Bristow," a voice said from behind him. Jack closed his eyes a moment, collecting himself, then did as he was told. He turned around to face two burly goons and two men who were clearly in charge of the situation. One was Kiyoaki Honda. The other, Jack noted with some surprise, was none other than Fan Li Kim, a squat little Korean man who looked like a less plastic version of his now deceased brother. The goon who had spoken gave a little nod, telling Jack to raise his hands. Jack complied. Kim laughed an ugly laugh.

"You've guessed, by now, that you've been poisoned," Kim hissed. "As we are the only possessors of the poison's antidote, you are at our mercy."

They don't realize APO has the antidote, Jack reasoned. *That's useful information.*

"Your cohort, Miss Santos, has been subdued outside," Honda added.

"You'll be coming with us, Mr. Bristow," Kim said.

"Where to?"

"A dry climate. It's good for the skin. Not that yours will be on your body for much longer, thanks to that poison. I hope you had your affairs in order when you last left Los Angeles. You won't be returning," Kim sneered.

"My only regret is that I had to sit through that one woman tonight singing 'I Will Survive,'" Jack said coldly.

"We should have had you sing that one," Honda chuckled. "The irony would have been so rich since you, Mr. Bristow, won't."

Jack tensed slightly, but betrayed no fear. "What do you want with me?"

"Nothing. Our issues are with an associate of ours, who seems unmotivated of late. We're hoping that offering him the chance to watch you die will prompt him to work a little harder. After all, you killed his father."

CHAPTER 16

JUST OUTSIDE LAS VEGAS
SHORTLY THEREAFTER

No one saw the explosion, because no one was inside. But if anyone had witnessed it, they'd have been impressed, particularly if they knew anything about precision demolition. The charges were perfectly placed, obliterating the beams that held the door in place and bringing down much of that entire wall, which was sent careening inward, collapsing with a loud crash over a set of desks and sending up an enormous cloud of gray dust. In the quiet aftermath of the explosion, the dust flitted through the air like a million tiny paper boats afloat on a gently undulating lake.

The quiet didn't last long. It was soon broken by a series of shouts and the stomp of approaching boots reverberating down through the newly opened hole.

A squad of men in helmets and black bulletproof armor emerged through the smoky doorway and took up positions all around the entrance, squatting and cocking their weapons, ready to quash any resistance from inside. The men were accustomed to doing this sort of thing in underground drug dens or the palatial lairs of arms dealers and warlords. But this time, when the smoke settled, a typical if completely deserted office, full of cubicles and desk calendars and slightly out-of-date laser printers, became visible. The men knew, however, that just because the room looked more likely to be defended by accountants with staple guns than thugs packing AK-47s, it didn't mean there was room for letting down one's guard.

"Interior appears clear," the leader of the squad barked gruffly into a comm on his wrist, but before he'd even finished speaking, a dark shadow emerged from the still-smoking hole in the wall, and a nattily dressed Arvin Sloane stepped into the office, kicking bits of rubble aside with his freshly polished shoes. His eyes made a circuit around the deserted room, and he was disappointed but not surprised by what he saw. Glancing back at the entrance, and taking a cursory inventory of the remnants of the hastily evacuated headquarters of Loge-21, Sloane couldn't help feeling a twinge of betrayal. After all, he'd stood just above this room in Paulson's cluttered office, unsuspicious and trusting in his old friend, completely unaware of what had been going on beneath his feet.

"Quite clever," he muttered with faint reluctance, before giving a nod to signal that the room was safe for the others to enter. The squad broke formation and began the task of sifting through the wreckage. Sydney and Vaughn entered the room a moment later. Both felt a bit overdressed, clad as they were in body armor, but there had been a hope that APO might beat Paulson to the punch and close in on Loge-21 before warning reached them. Obviously, that had not happened, and stepping into the vacant room felt oddly anticlimactic.

Vaughn strolled among the desks, marveling at the eerie emptiness of the place. He leaned down to pull at the exposed corner of a poster buried in rubble, and a soft-focus picture of a kitten clinging to a tree limb with one paw appeared. He dropped it before the slogan at the bottom of the picture became visible.

Sydney had stopped at one desk and was using her sleeve to wipe the dust off a framed photo left behind by one of the departed operatives. It featured a man in a fishing hat clutching the catch of the day, a sizable mackerel. He was surrounded by a wife and two cute-as-a-button kids. All four beamed. Sydney smiled wanly as she replaced the picture.

"I remember," she said, not so much to Vaughn as to the empty air, "I had a picture on my desk at SD-6. It was of me and Will and Francie. I remember finding it underneath all the rubble after we brought the place down. It's funny to think that spies are just people. No matter who they work for, good guys or bad, or something in between—they have hobbies, and families, and friends. . . ."

"Syd," Vaughn said suddenly, "I have something I want to talk to you about." He looked around tensely and happened to catch the eye of one of the armed men.

"Don't mind us," the man grunted.

Sydney suppressed a smile, but Vaughn wasn't amused. He cocked his head toward the entrance. Sydney nodded, and the two of them made their way back out along the walkway and through the trapdoor that had been concealed by a shabbily upholstered 1966 Corvair. APO had converted the greasy garage into a makeshift command center, and operatives buzzed about busily in accordance with Sloane's terse directives, taking notes and analyzing data. Sydney and Vaughn crossed through the chaos and, with the ring of a bell as they passed through the garage's entrance, into the desert outside, where they came to a stop just underneath the Paulson's Auto Body and Sales sign.

"Listen, if this is about how you kept the intel on Franklin a secret from me, I understand that you and my dad were just trying to keep me safe, and that you were just following—" Sydney began.

"No, Syd," Vaughn interrupted. He looked down guiltily, then continued. "Those pictures of your dad? The ones from Franklin's desk? They were taken in New Orleans on the day he killed Roger Thornhill. And they were taken by me."

Sydney drew back, her face creased in confusion and alarm. "I don't understand," she said quietly, after a pause.

"There was a time, not long after I met you, when I didn't trust Jack. I had been given this assignment to act as your handler, and when Jack asked me to come help protect you, of course I jumped at the chance. But he was a double agent, and he was so standoffish, and I barely knew him. . . . My bosses all told me he was trustworthy, but I wasn't sure, and you never know when you work in espionage. So I teamed up with another agent to keep tabs on him, off the books, so we'd have information in case he ever betrayed us. I don't even think I was worried about him betraying the country so much as I was afraid that he might betray you. So I documented him, photographing everything that went on in New Orleans."

"You must have been pretty slick to spy on my dad without him knowing it."

"I think I benefited from the fact that he thought I was too incompetent to worry about. Neither of us knew each other all that well back then," Vaughn said. "But not long after I took those pictures, I watched him kill Franklin's father. He didn't say anything, he didn't tell me that he knew Roger or that they had a history together, but I could tell he'd just done something that was very difficult for him. I could also tell he'd done it to protect you. That was when I knew that, however unorthodox his methods might be, he couldn't be a bad guy."

Sydney looked down modestly. Then she seemed to remember something and looked up, concerned. "But I don't get how the pictures ended up in Franklin's desk," she said.

"That other agent I teamed with? His name was Arnold Paulson."

"What?"

"I wish I hadn't given him the photos, Syd. If I hadn't, no one outside of the CIA would have ever known that Jack killed Roger. I can't tell you how much I regret it. I'm the reason why Franklin got involved with Keiko. And I'm the reason Dark Cloud knew to abduct Jack as leverage to make Franklin cooperate."

"But Franklin can't cooperate. We have him in custody. And you're also the reason Keiko is still alive. If Franklin hadn't been there to protect her . . ." Sydney trailed off.

Vaughn's mind was still on Jack and on his own past mistakes. "In order to save you, Jack left Franklin without a father. And in trying to keep you safe, I wound up giving information to the other side that led to Keiko being abused, and to Jack's being taken prisoner." He sighed, but it was inaudible due to the loud desert wind. "Sometimes our best efforts to protect the people we love wind up causing other people harm."

Sydney was thinking about how Franklin's beating the woman he loved had kept her from being targeted by Dark Cloud—how he'd both saved

Keiko's life and ruined it. "And sometimes the ways we hurt people wind up protecting them."

"I'm sorry I kept this from you, Syd," Vaughn said. She reached out and took his hand, then leaned in to kiss him. Vaughn knew he had been forgiven, but their reconciliation was interrupted by another tinkle of the bell as Marshall emerged from the garage, spotted them, and ran toward them, clutching a piece of paper in his hand.

"I've got it!" he cried, thrusting the page before them. It was a printout of a Loge-21 status report. It read "ERIC WEISS TRANSPORTED TO GOBI FACILITY."

"I pulled it off a damaged server," Marshall explained. "And yeah, I know we already knew Weiss was somewhere in the desert, but look at that!"

Marshall pointed at a series of numbers printed below the report. Both Sydney and Vaughn blinked twice, not sure what the importance of the sequence was.

"Those, guys," Marshall announced, obviously proud of himself, "are the latitude-and-longitude coordinates of the facility."

Sydney smiled. "Now we know where to go."

CHAPTER 17

THE CHINESE DESERT
THE NEXT DAY

The guard's name was Chen, and he hated his job. He would still hate it if it were more exciting. He would even hate it if he actually liked his coworkers. The fact that he'd never once had to use the rifle he'd been issued, and the fact that the only transmissions he'd ever sent over his radio were assurances that everything was quiet or discreet inquiries about what time the dice game was that night, were actually pluses. He certainly had no desire to shoot anyone or to live a life of action. His family needed the money, plain and simple, and if that scowling character who'd recruited him in a Shanghai back alley was willing to pay upward of eight thousand yuan a week to have him stroll around a deserted factory, well, Chen was more than willing to accept the cash, delivered regularly in sizable bundles that he always found ways to post off to his wife and kids, often bulked up (though occasionally much diminished) after an epic dice game.

The dullness of it all wasn't so bad. Mostly he hated his job because it was hot. Chen had attended business school briefly, in a dank second-story classroom run by a fly-by-night organization without accreditation of any kind, but even this meager excuse for an education had made him astute enough to realize that constructing a factory in the middle of the Gobi Desert was a boneheaded move. Forget the supply problems or the question of where to house your employees, and never mind the severe drain on your profits that came from having to transport your finished product to buyers who live on the other side of a vast and empty desertscape. The real problem was sand.

The sand ruins everything, Chen thought in Chinese, using his palm to balance his rifle on end while waiting for his shift to be over. *It ruins your equipment and creates a need for a huge maintenance staff that eats up a big portion of your operating budget. It's even the reason why it's so damn hot in here.*

Indeed, the ventilation system had long since succumbed to a slow and insidious onslaught by an army of granules of sand. The bosses still turned on the machines, figuring perhaps that their low hum might make people feel cooler even as temperatures swelled past stifling, but the sand-clogged system did little besides rattle like an aging chain-smoker wheezing for breath. Who knew what went on inside the vast network of shafts snaking through the factory's walls? *I sometimes feel as though this awful place is haunted by ghosts who might attack me from behind at any moment,* he once wrote superstitiously in a letter to his loving wife, describing the strange sounds he'd heard from the vents. He and the other guards had gotten so used to the noises that they no longer paid them much attention, but still, in addition to being swelteringly hot, the whole place was creepy. *Someday I'll start a business of my own,* Chen resolved as his hand trembled and his rifle tumbled to the floor.

And when I do, it'll be in a lush green neighborhood, surrounded by gardens, with no sand in sight.

Chen bent to pick up the rifle and straightened, ready to begin another balancing session, when to his surprise he found himself face-to-face with a masked man, dressed in stealth gear. "Forgive me the rudeness I'm about to commit," the man said in impeccable and very formal Chinese, even nailing the regional dialect, before slugging Chen hard in the face and leaving him unconscious on the floor.

A clatter overhead signaled Sydney emerging from the ventilation shaft. She dropped down beside the man. As she landed, she winced at the impact.

"Leg still bothering you?" Dixon asked as he pulled off his mask. "You know there's no one I'd rather have beside me here than you, Syd, but if you're not ready—"

"I'll be fine," Sydney said firmly. "I had to come. I really don't have anything to give my dad for Father's Day other than his freedom from the clutches of Fan Li Kim."

Dixon chuckled as he bound the guard securely

and lifted the keys from his pocket. "Thank you, Chen," he said to the unconscious man, reading the name off the ID tag on his chest.

Sydney did some quick recon to confirm that there were no more guards approaching from either direction, then spoke softly into a transmitter on her wrist.

"We're in position."

"Hold there, Phoenix," Vaughn replied with a calmness most people wouldn't be able to muster while being attacked by three armed men. "I'm experiencing a slight delay accessing the security room."

Nunchucks? he thought incredulously. *I mean, who actually uses nunchucks in this day and age?* And yet, here the three men were, whirling the traditional Asian weapons around with menacing agility like a high school flag squad with a mean streak. He'd dropped out of the ceiling into the middle of a quintet of guards, and though he'd taken two out with tranquilizers, that left these three, circling him with their chained clubs flying about.

The three men spread out to flank Vaughn. The agent lowered his center of gravity and prepared for an attack. But other than some technically impressive but ultimately pointless chucksmanship, the men made no move to strike. And that's when Vaughn realized what was going on: These guys had never actually attacked anyone before. They were probably just dudes who had seen a bunch of movies and practiced, unpartnered, their favorite onscreen ninja moves in their free time. They were good at looking tough, but they probably had no idea how to fight. To test his theory, Vaughn lashed out at one of them, who recoiled quickly in fear.

"All right, fellas," Vaughn announced, "I have things to do, so let's wrap this up." He swung at each of the other two, who both flinched, but Vaughn had apparently annoyed them enough that they finally lunged forward, their strength in numbers apparently assuaging their cowardice. Vaughn leaped up as the nunchucks swung toward him and grabbed the ventilation shaft he'd dropped from earlier. Swinging his legs up, he gripped the shaft with his heels and watched with amusement as his attackers' weapons tangled in one another and the men struggled to pull their individual nunchucks free of the chained-up mess. As they tussled over the useless nunchucks, Vaughn reached down and clunked two of the men's heads together, sending them crumpling to the floor. He then dropped down, subdued the last thrashes of resistance from the final guard, and bound each man up.

If it weren't so hot in here, he thought to himself, fishing in a pocket for gags to keep the men quiet, *I wouldn't have even broken a sweat.*

"Okay," he announced into his comm as he tightened the cuffs around the last man's wrists. "Almost ready. I'm heading into the security room."

"Good, Shotgun," approved Sloane from APO headquarters back in Los Angeles. "Keep us apprised of what you find."

He stood next to Marshall, listening intently to his agents in the field. The plan was to pincer in a three-man team, two agents roving while one accessed the security room so he could coordinate their movements. Marshall and Dixon had pored over blueprints and satellite scans to determine the best approach. The factory was in a kind of man-made oasis, a relic from a period of Chinese ambition to build in the Gobi Desert in vain hopes of industrializing the huge and otherwise empty land-mass. The complex of which the factory was a part had long since fallen into disuse, but satellite scans over the last few weeks revealed that it had been the site of activity that CIA observers could be forgiven for having mistaken for agricultural research. No one could have known that the research involved the creation of poison rain as a dress rehearsal for a full-scale attack on Tokyo.

It had been decided that the likeliest location for Jack, Nadia, and Weiss to be kept in captivity was the main factory building, and Sydney and Vaughn had entered through the ventilation system at the farthest, most desolate northeast corner of the building. As expected, security in this area was light, but the team anticipated stronger resistance as they approached their goals: the mechanical center of the factory where they thought the poison was being processed, and the administrative area beyond where Marshall guessed their fellow agents were being held.

"The access card we took off the guard is active," Dixon could be heard reporting, his voice crackling over the speaker. "We're moving west with caution."

Keiko was sitting at the table back at APO headquarters, and she leaned in to glance at the blueprints, imagining Sydney and Dixon sneaking their way through the harmless-looking blue and white hallways. Sloane had granted her permission to listen in on the operation, and he had turned a blind eye as she paged curiously through some declassified CIA protocol manuals while they waited for the team to be airlifted to the site. She'd read voraciously, giving free rein to her old grad student impulses to scan quickly, collecting information and gleaning important points. It was fascinating, the life of a spy, and Keiko felt oddly attracted to the idea of it.

"I've got Jack and Nadia on a monitor," Vaughn chimed in excitedly, and Keiko snapped to attention. "They're actually closer than we thought. The room they're being held in is just off the central mechanical complex. But there's no sign of Weiss or, uh . . ." There was a pause while Vaughn scanned the rest of the factory. Marshall looked sympathetically over at Keiko and gave her a reassuring smile, but both their faces fell when Vaughn added, "I'm sorry, Keiko, but I don't see any sign of your dad."

"Don't worry," Marshall offered. "We'll find him. This mission won't be a success unless we do."

Keiko nodded, looking over the blueprint version of the factory. She couldn't help noticing that every room, at least on paper, was completely empty.

With a series of hand signals, it had been decided that Dixon would move down along the wall of the central room until he reached Jack and Nadia, while Sydney carried the box with the antidote they'd brought, seeking out the stores of poison somewhere among the abandoned machines that filled the room's vast center.

"You're coming up on it, Outrigger," Vaughn told him, tracking his movements on the security cameras. "Evergreen and Raptor are in a room another hundred feet ahead of you. Watch for the two guards flanking the door."

I can handle them, Dixon thought to himself. *Dark Cloud obviously skimped a little on its security budget, if its guards are as easily dispatched as the one we met coming in.* He closed in on his target, then sprang out toward the door.

"These guys look a little tougher than the outer perimeter folks," Vaughn added.

"Probably should have told me that earlier, Shotgun," Dixon grimaced.

The two guards had their rifles raised, cocked and ready to fire when Dixon appeared. Each man weighed at least two hundred pounds, and they looked like their hobbies included lunching on tigers and bending steel bars with their bare hands.

Sydney, meanwhile, had found herself blocked off, and she could proceed only by squeezing through the large wheel of what she soon realized was an enormous R13-style turbine engine. She had an uneasy feeling that the engine could turn on at any minute, chopping her to pieces and spewing her out in a haze of exhaust, but after reaching out for the engine's hub, she fumbled blindly until she found the kill switch she knew was present on all R13s, and made sure it was locked in the "off" position.

Just one of the benefits of having a dad who sold airplane parts for most of my adolescence, she thought to herself. *Even if it did turn out he was up to something else entirely. . . .*

Once on the other side of the giant engine, she yanked the supply of antidote through the crawl-space and looked around, discovering to her astonishment that she was in a cleared-out central area of the complex, which opened up through gigantic hangar doors onto a runway visible outside. Crop dusters were all around her, with hoses leading from their tanks to six giant burbling vats that towered up above Sydney like skyscrapers. She stood up, then craned her neck back to gaze upward.

There were no lights on the cavernous room's ceiling. The tops of the vats, somewhere up in the unfathomable darkness above, weren't even visible.

"That is not going to be a problem," Marshall assured Sydney, even though he hadn't quite finished the calculations he was doing on a sheet of paper before him. He stopped, nervously chewed his pencil for a second, then added an extra line of calculus. There was far more poison here than APO had anticipated.

Sloane looked at him. Marshall seemed unusually hesitant, muttering rapidly under his breath, "She says each vat's height is approximately . . . and Bennett's Law of Chemical Interactions states that . . . so if we assume it's a Munson-grade polychloride base for the seeding compound . . ." Searching for someone to scowl at, Sloane turned to look at Keiko but found she was gone. Figuring she must have stepped out for some air after hearing that her father had yet to be located, Sloane turned impatiently back to Marshall.

"If you need to use the mainframe for your calculations . . ."

"No, no, Mr. Sloane," Marshall said. "She should be . . . I mean . . ." Marshall reached out and spoke directly into the comm. "Phoenix, you should be fine with the amount of antidote we sent along with you. Just barely. I assume they're storing the poison in tanks fitted with Gilchrist relays, so if you locate the intake valves and attach the pump, there should be just enough to neutralize it all."

There was silence, then the crackle of Sydney's voice: "The pump's attached, and the readout is dropping fast."

Marshall leaned back, visibly relieved. "That's the antidote running through the vats. Once it hits zero, the poison's no longer a threat."

Sloane placed a hand appreciatively on Marshall's shoulder. But he was less pleased with Marshall's skill in defanging the toxic substance than he was with APO's having foiled Paulson's plan.

You won't come out on top this time, Arnold, Sloane gloated silently, mentally addressing Loge-21's vanished leader. On his face was what, by Sloane's standards, passed for a satisfied smile.

* * *

"It's Dixon," Nadia announced as she peered through the tiny window in the door of the room where she and Jack were being held. "They found us!" She turned to look at Jack, who was leaning against the wall, trembling uncontrollably and gritting his teeth to keep himself from biting off his own tongue.

"They're actually . . . a little later than I expected," Jack gasped, struggling to keep himself together. The poison was working fast, playing with his mind, and making him lose focus quickly. Once Dark Cloud had discovered that Franklin had gone off the map—Jack could only hope that he was in APO custody—they had tossed his father's killer carelessly in this room, where despite Nadia's attempts to make him comfortable and keep him talking, Jack could feel himself drifting dangerously close to oblivion.

"Stay with me, Jack," Nadia urged.

Jack shook his head and pulled himself upright. "Have they gotten through . . . ?"

"Almost," Nadia assured him quickly. "We'll have help for you soon."

Jack clenched his fists, trying to will himself

into remaining conscious, while Nadia continued to watch closely through the window. For a moment, until he blinked and dispelled the illusion, Jack thought that she looked just like her mother.

ENTRY RESTRICTED, the door sign read. SECURITY LEVEL ONE OR HIGHER. Keiko grimaced, rattling the unyielding doorknob in frustration. *I spent close to six years married to the guy*, she thought. *Shouldn't I at least be able to talk to him if I want to?*

"Mr. Sloane said that your husband is not to have visitors," came a voice from behind her. Keiko spun around to discover an icy young woman—Tracy, was that her name?—urging her to give up on her attempts to see her imprisoned husband. "I'm sure you'll be able to talk to him once the operation is complete."

Keiko nodded, faking satisfaction. "I'm sure."

"You must be exhausted," Tracy said with a clearly fake brand of kindness. "Would you like a place to rest up a little? Or a beverage, maybe? I can have a colleague of mine get you whatever you need."

"No, no. I'm fine. Thank you, though."

Tracy pursed her lips, nodding, then proceeded on down the hall. Keiko turned to watch her go. Her eyebrows went up a little as she saw Tracy, in what the young woman probably thought was an unguarded moment, rub at a sore spot on her rear end.

Security level one, Keiko thought to herself. *That can't be very high. Even a junior-level agent like Tracy probably has that level of clearance.*

Keiko nonchalantly shadowed Tracy through the office, attracting no notice beyond a friendly little hello from one of the agents. Once, Tracy turned around abruptly as if she was worried she was being observed, but all she saw was Keiko, intently examining a picture of a former president on the wall. Shrugging off this apparent fascination with Bill Clinton's grin, and apparently reassured that no one was watching what she was doing, Tracy disappeared for a moment into a dark little corner of the office.

Pleased that she'd so skillfully evaded detection, Keiko bit her lip, unsure what to do next, but then Tracy emerged from the corner and departed. Glancing around to make sure no one was paying attention to her, Keiko crept into the corner as well, and found that this wasn't Tracy's office but—judging from the plaque prominently displayed on the desktop—belonged instead to some guy named Mark. A handwritten note had been placed on the computer keyboard; Tracy must have ducked in here to leave it. Curiosity got the better of Keiko, and she leaned down under the low ceiling to read the note.

"I got your little present," it read, "and believe me, I'll be showing you my full appreciation later on. —T."

Oh, how nice! Keiko thought happily. *I've stumbled across a little office romance! I wonder what the present was? What a sweetheart this guy must be! Well, Mark, maybe you can give me a little present too.* She sat down at the desk and tried to remember the tips she'd gotten from Nadia on rummaging through someone else's things. She was supposed to start with the trash, if she wasn't mistaken. In the garbage can under the desk were a few crumpled pieces of paper. Smoothing one of them out, Keiko found a photo of a man standing in an airport lounge, accompanied by printed-out text below.

"FACIAL RECOGNITION REPORT," the text began. "Prepared for Mark Baker, Junior Agent, Security Level One . . ."

Keiko smiled broadly. *Bingo,* she thought. *Now,*

let's see. I start with the things on top, then I go through the drawers. . . .

Sydney patted the syringes in her pocket, watching the readout dwindle to zero. She let out a sigh of relief at the thought that Dark Cloud's sinister plan had been foiled.

So this is how much poison it takes to eradicate an entire city, she reflected as she looked at the immense tanks before her. *Funny, but when you think of it that way, it doesn't really seem like that much at all.*

"Phoenix to Shotgun," she whispered. "Phase one is complete."

"Fantastic, Phoenix," came Vaughn's response. "Did you also take care of the poison in the . . ."

Sydney did not hear the rest. A hand had clamped over her mouth from behind her, and she was pushed forward and thrown to the ground. Her efforts to call for help failed to reach Vaughn, disappearing mutely into the muffling warmth of her attacker's silencing hand.

Dixon threw open the door, and Nadia immediately rushed out to meet him. She looked a little stunned as she surveyed the limp forms of the two guards.

"Wow, you made quick work of them," she marveled, nudging at one of the guards with her foot to confirm that he was out cold. Dixon was rubbing at the spot on his shoulder where the brawnier of the pair had managed to get a kick in before Dixon laid him out. The other one hadn't even managed to land a single punch.

Nadia helped Dixon drag the guards off to one side and bind their hands.

"Say what you will about SD-6's nefarious agenda," Dixon mused, "but they really knew how to train you in hand-to-hand." Dixon spotted Jack. His eyes grew wide with concern, and he ran to check the ailing agent's pulse.

"We need to get him to a doctor," Nadia said. "Unless . . . Jack says you have an antidote?"

"Sydney's got it," Dixon informed her, then spoke into his comm softly. "Outrigger to Phoenix. Raptor is in need of urgent medical attention. Can you come to—"

"Phoenix is in trouble," Vaughn interrupted urgently. "From what I'm seeing on the cameras, you'd better move fast." Dixon and Nadia exchanged glances, tacitly coming to a reluctant agreement that the best thing to do was to leave Jack where he was and bring the antidote back once they'd gotten it from Sydney.

"We won't be long," Dixon muttered, propping Jack up against the wall before following Nadia out. Jack forced open his eyes just long enough to glimpse the two dark, shadowy forms scrambling away from him.

Franklin, his head thrown back in the chair, was counting the number of ceiling tiles in the small interrogation room when a click from the door signaled that someone had run an access card through the security lock on the other side. Curious to see who'd been sent this time—he was sort of hoping that he'd eventually come face-to-face with Jack Bristow—he looked up, and was surprised to find his wife Keiko slipping into the room.

"Oh, honey! Thank goodness you're okay," she exclaimed, stepping inside and hurriedly shutting the door behind her. Franklin's eyes were locked on the access card in her hand, which she carelessly laid on the table off to one side before rushing over to him.

"Keiko, my love," he said without much

warmth. "So they've sent you in talk to me now? Tell them it won't work. I've said all I plan on saying."

"No, no!" she said, kneeling down solicitously at his side. "I snuck in. They don't know I'm here. I had to see you!"

"Forgive me, my love—you know I think the world of you—but I find it difficult to believe you've outwitted these people. You know, I think they might actually be with the CIA."

"Oh, Franklin! You really think they just handed me the key to your handcuffs?" Keiko dangled the key in front of his face. If he hadn't known his wife better, he might have thought her tone was a bit taunting. He eyed her for a moment, suspiciously.

"I think," he finally said, "that they gave you whatever they thought you'd need to gain my trust and get me to talk."

Keiko tut-tutted gently, standing and reaching behind him to unlock his shackles. As she leaned in, her hair fell across his face, tickling his skin, and if that was manufactured tenderness in the way she touched his wrists after freeing them, then Keiko was a far better actress than he'd given her credit for.

"Thank you," he said, eyeing her uncertainly. "But I still can't tell you any more than I've already told the others."

"Of course not," Keiko said gently, leaning back against the table. Franklin's lip curled a tad when his view of the access card was blocked by her body, but a moment later she began pacing the room. His eyes stayed locked on the card, still lying on the table. "After all, what else is there for you to tell, right? I read the report, and I understand, Franklin. I know you only hit me to protect me. I always knew that whatever you did, you did it out of love. Right, darling?"

"Right."

"And now you've explained everything, so I'm sure they'll let you go and we can go back to being very, very happy together. Right?"

"Of course. I'm sure that's what's going to happen." He wasn't looking at her as he said this, but Keiko seemed not to notice.

"I think they'll let us go soon. From what I can tell, you've already told them everything they could possibly want to know. Except, maybe . . ." She trailed off for a moment, looking at him with an intensity that threw him. "Except, maybe, about my dad. And you don't know anything about him, do you?"

"No." His focus shifted for just a moment from the card to his wife. "I don't. I'm not sure . . ."

Keiko seemed overjoyed to hear this, and she hugged him warmly. "I knew you wouldn't risk my father's life by keeping anything to yourself," she whispered as she embraced him.

His chin rested softly on her shoulder, and he could feel her breathing as she pulled him close.

Still his gaze remained locked, greedily intent, on the table behind her.

Sydney's attacker held her on the ground, and she could feel sweat dripping from his brow onto her neck as he pinned her in place. She writhed, attempting to squirm her way free, but this man was more skilled than the other, undertrained guards, and he seemed to predict her every move, finally bending her arm back to increase the pain and keep her from moving.

She found it strange, however, that he seemed to favor only his left arm and didn't use his right to hold her down. Tensing up and resolving to use this possible opening, she feinted left and then lunged right, feeling him lose his grip on her arm as she whipped around and turned the tables.

"Gotcha!" she exclaimed as she pressed his face into the factory floor, noting that indeed, his right arm was in a sling. She flipped him over roughly to discover . . .

"Eric!"

She released Weiss immediately, but he didn't move. He was drenched in sweat and was trembling severely, obviously wracked by the effects of the poison. Sydney fished in her pocket for the syringes and was deeply alarmed to discover that one of them had been smashed just now in the scuffle. She'd saved enough antidote to fill three syringes—for Jack, Nadia, and Weiss—but now only two were left. *This is no time to panic,* she said to herself, as she rolled up Weiss's sleeve and plunged the needle of one of the remaining syringes into his vein. His convulsions stopped almost immediately, and his muscles slackened until he lay limp on the floor.

"You're going to be okay, Eric," she murmured.

"I've been knocking out the guards . . . one by one . . . ," he gasped.

"That's great, Eric. You've done great work."

"And I've got to tell you about . . ." His voice,

already hoarse, gave out completely, but then he seemed to exert a tremendous amount of willpower, flailing like a fish on the floor until he was pointing urgently at a tiny walkway hidden in the shadows nearby. He coughed once, then faded away.

Sydney checked his pulse to confirm that he'd merely passed out, and limped her way over to the walkway. Poking her head through, her jaw dropped as she saw what Weiss had felt was so important to point out.

"I think we have a problem, guys," she intoned into her comm.

"We know," came Dixon's voice from nearby. "We just came through there." She spun around to find him and Nadia, out of breath, looking up at exactly what she was seeing.

"Um, Shotgun?" Nadia said blankly into the comm Dixon had given her. "We're going to need some input from Merlin on how to proceed."

"I take it," came Vaughn's voice through their earpieces, "that you've found the rockets."

CHAPTER 18

LOS ANGELES
SIMULTANEOUSLY

"Oh, yes! I remember that so well!" Franklin laughed heartily, reaching out to place his hand on Keiko's knee. The conversation had progressed to the point where now she was sitting in the chair, while he knelt before her devotedly. "We wound up at that little place in Malibu, didn't we?"

"I thought you looked so cute that night." Keiko sighed, letting the nostalgia wash over her. "Wearing that dark blue jacket, walking with me out along the beach . . . funny that we'd both come there with other people."

"What's funny is that I always told you I only went out with that girl—what was her name?"

"Laurie. She was a classmate of mine." Keiko smiled at the memory, enjoying the escape that reminiscing offered from the stress of the day.

"I always said I only went out with her so that I could get closer to you. And you always thought I was kidding, but . . . well, I think I've proven today that I meant it." The look on his face was one of supreme self-satisfaction.

Keiko smiled. "You were awfully cruel to her, using her like that. Such a sweet girl. She deserved better."

"She did all right, didn't she? You finally fixed her up with that guy you knew in the East Asian Studies Department, if I remember correctly. . . ."

"I'd been trying to set him up for ages! He was a hard one. But I hear they're still together. Chalk another one up for Keiko!"

Franklin stood, laughing, and strolled around the room as if stretching his legs, absentmindedly jingling the cuffs that Keiko had removed from his hands. "My little matchmaker. Well, it was a difficult task, anyway, but I finally got you." He paused, leaning casually against the table, his hands behind him to support his weight.

"Yeah, you got me." Her voice had a touch of darkness in it.

"I love remembering all the good times, darling. Things have gotten a little complicated since then, but . . . well, things always get complicated. Relationships are hard. We'll fix this."

"I hope so." Keiko looked down meekly. Then she glanced up, with pleading tears in her eyes. "I just hope I can fix whatever's happened with my father. You really don't know anything?"

Franklin leaned in, caressing her face and delicately wiping her tears away. "Darling, I promise you. I haven't spoken to him in . . ." He stopped himself, realizing he'd said too much.

"You've talked to him?" Keiko seemed importunate, even desperate.

"I . . . In an effort to coax information out of him . . . and to keep you out of harm's way . . . I once confessed my double loyalties to him, in secret. And it worked. He trusted me enough to reveal a few things that he never told Dark Cloud. Useful things."

"Really?" Keiko looked at him with admiration. "My, you must be a fantastic spy, Franklin." She pulled him to her and kissed him on the lips. Her mouth lingered over his for a long time.

"Keiko, darling," he said rapturously when she finally pulled away. He looked deeply into her eyes. "You have no idea . . ."

If Keiko noticed that the card was no longer on the table, she said nothing about it.

"So you're returning with the last of the antidote?" Vaughn asked, leaning over the microphone in the security room and watching Nadia weave adroitly through the maze of machinery.

"That's right," came her voice through his earpiece. "Fortunately, I wasn't exposed, which means having only one syringe left won't be a problem."

"Copy that. Get it to him quickly and hurry back. We're going to need all the hands we can get if the launch button is pushed on those rockets," Vaughn urged. He then turned sharply to look into the monitor that displayed the launch area. On the tiny black-and-white screen, the ten massive missiles, each loaded with more poison than had been in all the vats put together, dwarfed Sydney and Dixon, who crouched at the base of one of the launching pads inspecting the electronics inside. "What's your status, Outrigger?"

"This is all way over my head. Merlin, what have you got for us?" came Dixon's voice, tinged with stress.

"Describe for me one more time the outgoing leads on the launch mechanism," Marshall said. "You're telling me there are two, not three, red and white wires?"

"That's what I'm seeing," Dixon said. Vaughn could see Sydney holding an APO-issue flashlight, attempting to help Dixon peer into the dark panel.

"Okay, those are definitely remote launch sequencers," Marshall explained. "That means there's not a lot you can do from there. We can't neutralize the poison in the rockets, and we can't disable their launch abilities."

"We could just start hitting things with hammers," offered Sydney.

"No, no!" Marshall yelled, not realizing she wasn't serious. "That would be very bad. No, I just have to think this through."

"Shotgun! Come in, Shotgun!"

Vaughn spun around and returned to Nadia, whom he was startled to find calling to him and spreading her arms helplessly as she stared at the security camera trained on the room where they'd left Jack. "What's wrong, Evergreen?"

"Jack's gone!"

Vaughn barely had time to process this information before he felt something prodding into the back of his neck. Recognizing it was the barrel of a gun, he stiffened, and a gloved hand reached around him to switch off his comm. Cut off from the other agents, Vaughn was turned slowly around to find Kiyoaki Honda, backed by several armed thugs.

"Missing someone, are you?" Honda asked as he callously ripped out the electronic innards of the APO comms system. "Perhaps we can help you find him."

I'm moving. My legs aren't propelling me, but I'm moving. My legs are dragging, in fact. I'm not walking, not going somewhere because I want to. I'm being taken there. That can't be good.

"Heavy, isn't he?"

That's Chinese the man is speaking. Where am I, again? Somewhere in China, it appears. The desert? Is that right? Vague recollection: I was brought against my will from Tokyo to the Chinese desert. With whom? Memory isn't entirely clear. With Sydney? With Irina? What's going on?

"These Americans, they're all heavy. It's all the fast food they eat."

"Wish we could just kill him. It'd be easier than dragging him like this. But if Mr. Kim says he's to be kept alive, he stays alive."

I need to pull my thoughts together. I'm in China. I was brought here with Nadia. I need to stop Fan Li Kim from launching an attack on Japan. Also, whatever I do, I must apprehend Kiyoaki Honda, because he made me sing. No one makes Jack Bristow sing.

"This room's the one, isn't it? Got the key?"

"Right here."

They're opening the door, pushing me through. I need to catch myself, if I can, before I hit the . . .

Too late. That pain I just felt, that was concrete. But concrete is kind of nice, once my body settles into it. Hard and cold, but oddly comforting, kind of like Roger used to say he imagined death would feel. I wonder if that's how it felt for him, when I killed him. . . .

"Jack?"

Who's that? Who's speaking now?

"Jack, wake up. It's Vaughn. They've got us in some sort of holding cell in the administrative area.

We need to get out, get you the antidote that Nadia's carrying, and stop the rocket launch."

Vaughn? That useless kid who brought a camera, of all things, to a New Orleans cemetery on a crucial off-the-books op, like some sort of tourist? No: That was a long time ago. I'm mixing up time. That's something the poison's doing to me. Vaughn has proved himself since then, and I know it. I need to listen to him: Pull myself off the floor, sit up, scan the room, and come up with options for escape.

"Good, Jack. Stay with us. We need to make a plan."

"Us, Vaughn?" *I sound terrible, but at least I can still talk.* "Who else is here?"

Look around the room: almost empty, except for a table and two chairs, another ventilation shaft, and a man. Who is he? Asian features, light complexion, probably Japanese. Bookish, spectacled. He looks like he was once quite built, but he's wasted away. What's wrong with him? He's trembling and moaning, lying there on a cot, sweating: Probably the effects of the poison.

I need to focus. Find it in myself and make myself speak: "Who's the other man?"

"I'm pretty sure that's Hikaru Terajima. And he's even sicker than you."

"I can't believe my dad told you all that," Keiko marveled, her hands continuing to caress Franklin's face lovingly. "With those codes, you could avert Dark Cloud's attack from anywhere in the world!"

"Yes, I suppose so." Franklin was enjoying the attention, speaking in dreamy tones as though he were a thousand miles away from this cramped little holding cell. "Knowledge is power in the spying world, my dear, so I've kept this to myself. I haven't even told my superiors at Loge-21."

"Shouldn't you tell Sydney and the other people here?" Keiko asked, wide-eyed.

"Oh, I'll tell them. But why be so forthcoming now? Why not wait until we're free? You were planning on sneaking me out of here, weren't you?" There was a glimmer in Franklin's eye, one that seemed to frighten Keiko.

"I don't know, Franklin. I just wanted to see you. . . ."

"How were you going to sneak me out? I'm sorry. I mean, how were you going to sneak us out? Surely you thought about it." He peered at her, and she felt like his eyes could bore right through her. Keiko's voice began to quaver, just as it had so many times before, when he'd intimidated her into doing anything he said. A smile played over Franklin's face as he recognized that he had her right where he wanted her.

"I . . . there's . . . we were going to go out of this room, turn right, and sneak down to the end of the hall, where the card would get us through an unguarded exit. But why do that? Why not just tell them what you know? They'll release you once they realize you're on their side."

"Because, my dear," Franklin said simply, "the fact of the matter is, I'm on no one's side but my own." Taking her hands in his with a sudden, sharp movement, he gripped her wrists fiercely and pulled her arms back around the chair, snapping the cuffs onto them and pinning her in place. Keiko went white, her body tensing uselessly against the restraints.

"What are you doing?"

"Keiko. darling, I've saved your life so many times. Just this once, save mine."

"Why can't I come with you?"

"You'd hold me back." He leaned in and kissed her, his face downright happy. He held up the card in his hand. "But I appreciate your getting me this. It's my ticket to freedom."

"Wait! You've always said you couldn't live without me!"

Franklin stood and went to the door, opening it and looking out stealthily. He turned back to her and whispered before he disappeared out into the hall.

"I expect," he said, the smile vanishing from his face and leaving nothing but cold calculation, "that like a lot of people who've used that phrase, I will be pleasantly surprised when I discover it's untrue."

And then he was gone. Keiko didn't shout or cry. If anything, she seemed vaguely pleased.

Suddenly, Dixon could see. It wasn't, however, because Sydney had found the right angle for shining the flashlight. It was because the entire room was instantly ablaze with hundreds of spotlights, and a million tiny readouts all over the launch mechanism came to life and began spouting out countdown information, whirring and clicking and emitting an ominous electronic ringing noise. When a tiny entry terminal lit up before his eyes, prompting him to input "CODE #1," Dixon was so startled that he jerked quickly back from the panel he'd been peering into.

"What's going on?" he demanded, looking anxiously at Sydney, who was obviously as baffled as he was.

"That was the beginning of the end," announced Fan Li Kim as he strode through the walkway with a squad of armed guards. "We've initiated the launch sequence. Soon the Japanese capital will be drenched in poison, and the world will know that a similar rain of death could fall at any time. None of our political, or financial, demands will ever fail to be met again."

Sydney and Dixon got to their feet, their hands held in the air. From nearby they could hear the sputtering of airplane engines being started. "You're launching the crop dusters, too?" Sydney asked, shouting over the distinctive sound of a plane taxiing out of the factory and onto an outdoor runway.

"That's the sound of a little squall that's going to eliminate you and all but the most essential people here at this factory. We're covering our tracks. Too bad that means you won't be around to hear the full-fledged storm that will rage over Tokyo."

Sydney exchanged a brief glance with Dixon, one that translated to: *They don't know I've neutralized the poison in the dusters.*

"Is that a look of concern for my welfare?" asked Kim. "Not to worry! My lieutenants and I have been treated with an antidote. The rain that falls here will kill everyone but us. Please don't tell the guards, though. None of them speak enough English to understand what I'm telling you. Not that they'd believe you anyway. But I'd hate to upset them, when they have so little time left."

"How long until the rockets launch?" Dixon asked. His voice sounded steely.

"Fifteen minutes. I wish I had time to show you Dr. Terajima's rocket designs, which are really quite wonderful. We couldn't have done it without him. His cooperation was difficult to secure, but when we finally told him yesterday that we'd kill his daughter, he was upset enough to supply us with the last few crucial details. We told him afterward that we killed her anyway, for good measure."

"Keiko's not dead," Sydney insisted.

"When we didn't hear back about the cell phone, we assumed you'd stopped our man Franklin from carrying out that last stage of the plan." Kim shrugged. "But what her father doesn't know won't hurt him."

* * *

Jack, struggling against the mental effects of the poison, helped Vaughn hold Keiko's father down and check his vitals. He could feel his own pulse skittering around as Vaughn felt for Dr. Terajima's.

"I managed to get a few words out of him before you arrived, Jack. He actually administered the poison to himself, plunged his hand in a jar of the stuff and left it there, soaking it up. He believes his daughter was killed by Dark Cloud, and he feels like he has nothing left to live for."

"You . . . you told him that she's alive?" Jack asked. He swallowed, trying to hold himself together.

"Yes. But he didn't believe me. He assumed I was another double or triple agent like Franklin, and he didn't trust what I was saying." Vaughn fell quiet as he pressed his ear to Dr. Terajima's chest. "He won't last long."

Jack turned, with difficulty, and scanned the room. The ventilation shaft looked securely bolted to the wall. He was contemplating smashing the table and chairs, maybe even the cot, and using the debris to break down the door, when Vaughn perked up his ears. Jack listened too; they could make out the sound of footsteps approaching.

"This the one?" they heard a female voice saying

in Chinese from out in the hall. An affirmative grunt was followed by a loud "Oof!" and the thud of a falling body. Then the door clicked as it was unlocked, and Nadia appeared. With a shove of her foot, she used the body of the knocked-out guard to prop the door open.

"These guards are remarkably helpful," she said, "if you make it clear that you're capable of crushing their windpipes with your bare hands."

Vaughn looked relieved as Nadia rushed in, knelt down, and began fishing through her pockets. Jack, however, eyed the downed guard warily. "I think," he gasped, "that that's the man who implied I was overweight."

"Not a nice thing to say about a dying man," Nadia said, drawing a glare from Vaughn. "I can joke about that because I brought this." She produced the syringe. "Roll up your sleeve, Jack."

Vaughn began helping her expose Jack's arm, when suddenly Jack's hand clamped over Vaughn's, stopping him.

"How many doses are there?" Jack asked.

Nadia looked uncertainly at Vaughn, then answered, "This is the only one left, Jack."

Jack's head rolled back limply, then he pulled

himself to a sitting position. He extended a shaky finger out toward Dr. Terajima's limp form.

"You're going to need him to stop the launch," Jack said. "Give the antidote to him."

As Vaughn and Nadia exchanged uneasy looks, the low rumble of thunder could be heard from outside.

Mozart's own fingers, cascading over pianofortes as he performed his music in Austrian salons, could not possibly have moved with such confident fluidity as Marshall's did over his computer keyboard. He pored over the screen with the kind of squint that movie heroes reserve for staring down villains, and even the hot and unpleasant breath of Arvin Sloane looming over his shoulder couldn't distract him from the task at hand.

"The disruption of communications, coinciding so closely with the initiation of the launch sequence, can only mean our agents have been compromised," Sloane hissed.

"That's probably true," Marshall responded, absently.

"I assume you're investigating an electronic back door to the launching or targeting systems."

The *clickety-click* of the keys remained steady and smooth as Marshall nodded affirmatively. "Dr. Terajima designed a rather brilliant operating system for the rocket capacitors. My guess is he was trying to make it complicated, looping bits of code through each other in order to confuse the people who were forcing him to make it. But if you just sift—"

"Sift?"

"Yes, Mr. Sloane. If you just remove, bit by bit, all the smaller pieces of code, then the longer, more complex ones remain. And they're the ones we're looking for. Now that's interesting . . ." He trailed off, tilting his head to ponder a thorny couple of lines on the screen.

The door opened, and Mark poked his head into the room. "Mr. Sloane, sir?" Sloane silenced him with a look, then turned back to Marshall.

"What have you found, Marshall?"

"I can't be absolutely certain, but I think there's a fail-safe abort process built into the launch sequence. But it's going to require maybe three codes, of indeterminate length." He punched in a set of commands, looking uncertain about it as he did so. "I'm tasking our best code-breaking processors to work on it, but the codes could be thousand-digit numerical sequences, or something as simple as Dr. Terajima's dog's name. This could take weeks."

"I'm guessing we have a matter of minutes, so that is not an option," Sloane said icily, before turning back to Mark. "What is it, Baker?"

Mark cleared his throat. "I just came to inform you, sir, that satellite imaging has gone offline on the desert facility. The cloud cover is thickening, and apparently it has started to rain."

Sloane's eyes narrowed, but he snapped back when Marshall made an excited announcement: "I've got the first code, sir! It's the oldest trick in the book! It's his daughter's name! It's 'KEIKO'!"

Nadia unlocked yet another door, then poked her head in to find yet another empty office. "Not in here, either," she reported.

Vaughn, struggling to support Dr. Terajima's dead weight, set his teeth in frustration. "I don't like leaving Jack alone for this long. Are you sure this will work?" he asked, his tone giving away that he wasn't at all convinced.

"We did our best to revive him, but I think he's too emotionally battered. We need something big, the psychological equivalent of dousing him with cold water. Let's try this room." She tried the guard's master key in the last door along the grimy hallway, but it jiggled uselessly in the lock. "I guess they don't want the guards coming in here. That's a good sign," Nadia muttered, backing up and bashing in the door with a fierce kick. It didn't give way easily, but it was no match for Nadia.

Impressed, Vaughn followed her inside, setting Dr. Terajima down on a filthy but serviceable couch in one corner of a sparsely furnished apartment. Nadia hurried over to a desk in one corner, eyeing a telephone.

"This looks like Honda's quarters," Vaughn mused, examining some documents on a small table next to the couch and reading through the Japanese names in the addresses.

"Doesn't really matter whose name comes up on the caller ID," Nadia said as she fished through her pockets.

"What are you looking for?" Vaughn asked. "You don't remember APO's phone number?"

"I'm not calling APO," Nadia replied. "Aha!" She produced a business card and flipped it over to dial a number handwritten on the back.

As Nadia listened to the dull ring through the

receiver, Vaughn began to look around the apartment. *Surely Honda has something in here that we could use. . . .*

"I've been held prisoner before," Sydney said flatly, listening to the pitter-patter of rain beginning to fall on the factory's roof. "Evil geniuses once harvested my eggs against my will, so suffice it to say that having my hands and feet duct-taped doesn't impress me much."

She and Dixon were trussed up on the floor not far from the launch platform. Her efforts to mouth off to Kim had thus far failed to annoy him into making some crucial mistake, but Dixon still appreciated her trying. Kim's fierce glares in response prevented him from detecting the tiny motions Dixon was making with his legs as he sawed the tape on his feet against a piece of machinery. He'd cut halfway through the tape already. He planned on making his move any minute.

"The things you do in your personal life, Miss Bristow," Kim said offhandedly, "do not interest me at all." He turned to welcome back his associate, who emerged, sniveling, from the darkness. "Mr. Honda, procurer of the antidote!" he announced grandly. "We're ten minutes from launch. What on earth has taken you so long?"

Honda froze in place, spreading his arms apologetically. "Prisoners," he replied. "They're a vexing bunch."

"Indeed they are. Come see the new ones we've gathered over here! Would you believe, another Bristow? We should really try to track down the mother. You fetch far more on eBay for a complete set."

Honda looked unamused and made no move to approach Kim. Sydney, watching his eyes, realized what was going on before anyone else, and she nudged Dixon with her elbow. He'd been concentrating on cutting the tape on his legs, but he looked up and quickly understood.

"Ready when you are," he whispered, and she nodded.

Kim detected the strange attitude in his cohort a touch too late, and his guards were, as always, slow in responding. Suddenly a hand appeared out of the dark, grabbing Honda's shoulder and shoving him aside, and Jack Bristow was revealed, clutching Honda's gun and doing an impressive job of controlling his shaking hand. Once he'd been left alone by Vaughn and Nadia, sheer will had carried

Jack out and into the halls, where he'd found and subdued Honda, before forcing him into this ruse. It was clear despite the tremors that a bullet fired from the gun in his hand would hit its mark, or come close enough.

"Guards!" Kim cried, but Jack had already crouched, sent a knife he'd lifted from Honda skidding across the floor to Sydney's feet, and fired a fusillade of bullets as cover. Kim groaned, diving to the side, as Dixon ripped the tape on his feet apart and sprang up, quickly taking out three guards by kicking them to the floor despite having his hands still bound.

"Dixon!" Sydney called out, having freed herself by cutting the tape with the blade. She held it out, and Dixon backed into it, freeing his own hands as Jack dove across the floor, firing all the while, sending the guards scrambling for cover.

"Everyone . . ." Jack was struggling for breath. "Everyone okay?"

"Better than you," Sydney said, concerned. "What happened to the antidote Nadia was bringing you?"

"Repurposed," Jack replied succinctly through gritted teeth.

"Sydney!" Dixon cried from his position at the

access panel. "It looks like there's a series of codes that have to be entered to stop the launch. I'm assuming they were programmed by Keiko's father. Someone's already input the first one: it's 'KEIKO.' It's asking for the second."

"You could ask Dr. Terajima," Jack gasped, placing a bullet neatly in the shoulder of a guard across the room. "Vaughn and Nadia . . . are trying to revive him as we speak."

Sydney had grabbed a gun and was joining her father in fending off the attacking guards. "If the first code was the name of his daughter, try his wife's name for the second. Maybe 'MIDORI.'"

Dixon typed, then smiled warmly as he read the terminal's response: "CODE ACCEPTED. INPUT CODE #3." "That's it, Syd! Come up with the last one, and we're home!"

But Sydney could think of nothing more that she knew about Keiko's family. If only there were a way to ask her!

There was a kind of peace to sitting alone in the interrogation room. Keiko was enjoying it, reveling in the serenity of her first moments truly free from Franklin. She had to say she was quite content indeed, despite the discomfort of having her hands bound. It helped that she knew the quiet wouldn't last long.

But the interruption to her happy thoughts came in a different form than she expected. It came in the form of her own shriek.

She felt her phone vibrating in her pocket. *You'll have to wait, caller, whoever you are,* she thought. But then she remembered that the ringing phone wasn't hers. She'd left her cell in her purse, in the other room. This phone was the one she'd retrieved from the package sent to Franklin by his Dark Cloud cohorts—it was her father's. Suddenly she wanted desperately to answer it.

"Hold on!" she cried out pointlessly to the caller, who obviously couldn't hear. She struggled, flailing in place, her arms pinned to the chair's back painfully.

Finally she stopped, breathing hard. She needed to come up with a plan.

"What would Sydney do?" she found herself asking aloud. She gazed around the room, looking for something she could use to solve the problem at hand. "Focus, Keiko. That's what she'd do. Focus. And . . ." Keiko set her jaw with determination. "She'd do whatever she had to."

Shouting like a shot-putter and shaking in her seat as she concentrated all her energy in her legs, Keiko threw the chair back in place, pushing up and out with her feet to send herself careening backward against the interrogation room wall. She did this three or four times, each time hurling herself with more force, until finally the chair tipped over and fell, clattering against the floor and breaking in six or seven pieces. To Keiko it felt like parts of her body were breaking as well, but she was able to pull her cuffs free of the broken chair back, and by slipping them under her heels she brought them, still bound, in front of her. With a pained grin, she pulled the phone out of her pocket and answered.

"Hello, hello?" Keiko was high on endorphins and self-assertion. "Who is this?"

"Keiko! It's Nadia! Thank goodness you gave me your father's cell phone number. Here, I'm going to put you on the phone with him!"

"No, don't!" Keiko insisted unexpectedly. "I have to tell you the secret codes to stop the rocket launch! I got them from Franklin before he escaped."

"What?" Nadia sounded horrified. "Franklin escaped?"

"Don't worry," Keiko said confidently. It was an

incredible bit of timing that at just that moment, the sound she'd been expecting rang blaringly from out in the hall. Keiko smiled when she heard the alarm bell. "I don't think he'll get far."

Franklin had congratulated himself on the skill with which he'd extracted an escape plan from his naive wife and on the stealth he'd shown in creeping slowly, patiently down the APO hallway, concealing himself completely each time someone passed by. He'd been sad to have to leave Keiko behind: He truly believed he loved her. *But even love breaks down in the face of self-preservation,* he told himself, believing that even more.

He'd finally reached the end of the hallway when he produced the card he'd taken from the table. Snapping it gleefully with his fingers, he ran it smoothly through the lock on the exit, which he'd found unguarded, just as Keiko had promised. There was a moment as he waited for the little light on the lock to turn green. He could almost taste his freedom. *I'll miss you, Keiko darling,* he addressed her in his mind, *but I expect you'll get along fine without me.* That was the last thing that would cross his mind before any hope he'd nursed of ever seeing daylight again was abruptly and loudly dashed.

The ringing of the alarm bell threw Franklin for a considerable loop. *Didn't I see Keiko use this card to get into the interrogation room? It worked fine for her!* That was when he turned it over in his hands and saw that he was holding Keiko's Blockbuster card. *What? How could she have switched them?* A memory struck him, of his wife crossing in front of the table, leaning back on it casually, blocking his view for a mere instant, just as he'd done a few minutes later when he lifted the switched card, thinking she hadn't suspected a thing. *Never marry a graduate student,* he told himself with a resigned smile. *They learn fast.*

Agents swarmed in, some with drawn guns, and Franklin lay compliantly on the floor, locking his fingers behind his head as instructed. The look on his face was steely as he gazed down the hall he'd just traversed. The bell was still ringing as he watched Keiko emerge from the interrogation room, clutching a cell phone to her ear, her hands still cuffed. A confused-looking APO agent unlocked her cuffs, and as he was freeing her Keiko looked back, her eyes locking with Franklin's when she spotted him on the floor.

She looked frantic, in a tremendous hurry, but still she took a moment to pluck her wedding ring off her finger and roll it, like a bowling ball, down the hall. It rolled tinnily over the tiles until it bumped Franklin squarely in the forehead, tipped over, and fell, rattling noisily as it settled right before his eyes.

When the countdown reached two minutes, a massive rumbling noise sounded, and the roof of the factory swung open to allow the missiles room to launch. Water had begun to pour onto the machinery, soaking everything, and lightning could be seen outside, striking barren sand as a rainstorm raged over an arid desert. Many of the guards took flight—rumors must have reached them that the rain was poison—and Jack made a heroic charge to send them back through the walkway and into the central hangar area. He was unsteady on his feet, but even operating at ten or fifteen percent, Jack Bristow was a formidable force. Most of the attacking squad wound up cowering for cover, unsure whether to be more afraid of the rain or of Jack.

Jack was lowering his weapon, ready to collapse, when he caught a glimpse of Honda, who was trying to flee by wiggling his way through a cramped crawlspace between some still blades. Jack pursued him, throwing himself down on his stomach to crawl along behind him.

"Give up, Honda!" Jack cried. "There's still time to stop this launch!" His fingers had found purchase on the cuff of Honda's pant leg, and Jack had him covered with the pistol in his other hand.

"Tokyo's a city no one will miss," Honda grunted, before pulling off one of the luckiest bits of desperation fighting Jack had ever seen. A flailing kick backward knocked the gun out of Jack's hand, sending it careening up along the curved wall of the crawlspace. The gun slowed as it slid up the wall, then fell back down, coming to a stop just inches ahead of where Honda was crawling.

What is this round room? Jack asked himself, looking around and feeling an odd sense of recognition. *Is this an engine? I swear I've seen one of these before. . . .*

For his part, Honda was awed at his good fortune for a moment, but then reached out and grasped the gun, wriggling around to point it at Jack's head. "And I doubt anyone will miss you, either," he said, his finger tightening around the trigger.

A bullet did fire from the gun, but by the time

it did, much of Honda had already been sliced off his body. Jack had reached out and thrown the kill switch on the R13 engine, using every last ounce of his strength to pull himself back out of the turbine before its blades began to turn. Gasping for breath and feeling the poison sap his energy, Jack listened as the bullet from the gun ricocheted repeatedly within the roaring engine's confines, and watched as Honda was reduced to a fine red spray. He grimaced slightly at the gruesomeness of the sight.

Not even a man who made me sing deserves to die like that, Jack thought, as he slipped into unconsciousness.

Sydney had followed Kim as he'd fled up a long spiral staircase that led him through the open launch panels in the ceiling. When she emerged after him onto the rain-soaked roof, she could hear him laughing happily. Squinting through the fierce gusts, she could make him out a few feet away, clinging to a radio antenna and pointing at her mockingly.

"And what has you so amused?" she asked, wiping her brow so she could see more clearly.

"The fact that after this is over," Kim cackled,

"all I'll need is a towel, while you're going to be needing a stretcher! I'm immune, thanks to the secret stash of antidote Honda obtained for us, but you, you're covered in poison rain!"

Yeah, yeah, Sydney thought, *poison rain.* She used her hand to cover her eyes as she surveyed the terrain. Cables ran all over the roof, and the launch panels had rotated more than ninety degrees, leaving sharp slopes that swept down to gaping holes where the missiles were to emerge. Thunder rolled angrily all around, its low claps harmonizing unpleasantly with Kim's high-pitched giggling. *What the hell,* she decided. *Here goes nothing.*

Charging forward, Sydney leaped over one of the huge holes in the roof and landed on the other side, splashing down mere feet from Kim. His laughter stopped abruptly, and he looked her up and down.

"Nice jump," he said frankly, then tore away across the roof.

"I need you to stop the launch sequence, Kim!" Sydney cried, chasing him through the puddles. "Tell me the third abort code!"

"Code?" Kim cried. "I have no idea what you're

talking about!" But he stopped, dropping down and extending a leg to trip Sydney up. She went tumbling into one of the wet sloping surfaces as Kim grabbed one of the cables and lunged at her, wrapping it savagely around her neck and trying to choke her with it. She tensed under the pressure on her esophagus, struggling to stand but finding that although she managed to make contact between the wet roof and her boots, she couldn't bring her weakened leg to pull her upright.

"I never even liked my brother all that much, you know," Kim hissed in her ear. "But I'll still enjoy killing his killer."

Sydney felt things start to go black. The lack of air was starting to cut away at her field of vision. Her head lolled down, and within her tiny and diminishing circle of sight her eyes locked in on her feet, wedged against the sloping roof as one hand grasped an antenna and the other grappled weakly with the cable around her neck. *Are these black boots going to be the last thing I ever see?* she wondered. *I always imagined things ending more spectacularly.*

But then a memory raced through her mind. If there hadn't been an evil Korean man trying to strangle her, she might even have smiled. She released her grip on the antenna and focused all her might toward straightening her knees, bringing her to an unsupported standing position, her feet firmly planted on the wet, sloping roof. However, as Sydney knew from experience, APO stealth boots have almost no tread on wet surfaces, and her feet slid right out from under her.

Kim was taken aback as the girl he was choking seemed to be slipping away, and he threw himself toward her. The two of them tumbled painfully down the roof toward the launch aperture. Sydney had known what would happen and reached out to grasp the cable. Kim had not, and with a terrified cry, he went down and over the edge, falling to his death far below.

The sickening crunch of his body as he hit the concrete floor of the launch area awakened Weiss, who'd been passed out a few feet away. He foggily registered what had just happened.

"Man, those Kim brothers," Weiss muttered to himself. "Their worst enemies are the Bristows and the force of gravity."

As Keiko burst into the crowded communications room, Marshall was sputtering out reassurances to

Dixon. "We're going to come up with the third code! I just need a little more time."

"Marshall, the countdown's reached sixty seconds," Dixon could be heard uttering, trying to restrain his own unease with the situation.

"I know the code! I know it!" Everyone turned to stare at Keiko. "It's 'SHIGEO NAGASHIMA'! He's Dad's favorite baseball player!"

Marshall's fingers typed in the name with lightning speed. Everyone held their breath, Marshall's knuckles went white, and even Sloane clenched the fist he was leaning on. A moment passed, and then Marshall shook his head grimly.

"It's not accepting the code."

"No good from this terminal, either," Dixon added.

Keiko's mouth dropped open. "But that's what my dad told Franklin!" She spoke desperately into the phone. "Nadia, did you say my dad is there? Let me talk to him! Daddy? Daddy?"

Marshall punched some keys, and the cell connection could be heard over the speaker. Keiko's father, still struggling to emerge from unconsciousness, could be heard groaning, his voice sounding faint. "Is that . . . is that my daughter?"

"Daddy, it's me! It's Keiko! We need your help stopping the—"

"It's not you. You're not her." He sounded oddly revitalized by his refusal to believe her. "They killed her. My darling girl, they beat her for years and then they . . ." Everyone in the room, save Sloane, seemed faintly embarrassed at hearing this painful, tender moment. Marshall began to regret enabling the speaker.

"No, Daddy! They lied to you! I'm fine, and I'm with good people, people who are trying to stop those men. We need your help!" Keiko's face was concentrated, unwavering.

"Why should I believe you? So many lies, and lies about other lies, and your husband, if it's really you, wasn't really bad, and I told him things and then he killed you. . . ."

"No, Dad. Listen to me. Franklin told me the codes. He said they were my name, and Mom's name, and Shigeo Nagashima's name." Keiko couldn't help smiling a little at reciting her dad's three favorite people. "I must be Keiko. Otherwise, how could I know that?"

"You could be pretending to be her, to get the codes to do something awful. . . . I just can't . . ."

Keiko's eyes glanced over at the countdown as her father paused.

"Dad, we have, like, fifteen seconds. If the third code isn't your favorite baseball player, who is it?"

"I wanted . . ." Dr. Terajima was audibly fighting off tears. "I wanted to throw people off, so I made the third code the name of my least favorite person in baseball, not my favorite. If you're really my daughter, you'll know who that is. . . ." He trailed off and began to sob.

Keiko, however, just smiled. "Oh, Daddy," she said, her eyes growing wet with happiness. "Why would you let someone as awful as Don Nomura be the savior of Tokyo?" And she broke into laughter as the stillness in the room gave way to a bustle of phone calls and frantic typing.

"That's it!" Marshall announced, watching the terminal spout out the code's acceptance and signal the termination of the launch sequence. "'DON NOMURA!' That's it!"

Indeed, when Sloane leaned in to look, he could read the words "LAUNCH ABORTED" on the screen. He slumped down in his chair and exhaled, just like everyone else, though he did it somehow less pleasantly.

But Keiko had nudged Marshall, who nodded and turned off the speakerphone, and she was happily, tearily conversing with her father, who was just as happy and tearful on the other end of the line. "Daddy, once you get home," she could be heard saying tenderly, "I promise to make you the finest cup of tea you've ever tasted."

Vaughn sprinted out of Honda's office and raced through the factory hallways. He'd memorized the factory's layout, but once he reached the mechanical area he had to duck through tight spaces and weave past bulky crates and slabs of metal, even detouring at one point when he found the only route forward was through a puddle of blood and an immense whirring engine. But finally he turned a corner and saw Jack, collapsed and unconscious.

"Jack!" Vaughn cried, kneeling down next to him and rolling up his shirt sleeve before producing a syringe and jabbing it almost blindly into Jack's arm. The liquid moved down the needle and into Jack's blood, and then all Vaughn could do was wait.

A long time passed. It was probably only a matter of seconds, but it felt like a long time. And then Jack slowly opened his eyes. Vaughn grinned and answered Jack's question before he could ask.

"I searched Honda's office and found the additional antidote he'd stockpiled. I think we got it to you just in time."

"And Sydney? Is she safe?"

"Yes, Dad," Sydney replied. She stepped forward, sopping wet but in one piece. She grasped his hand warmly. "I'm fine."

"That's good. Vaughn," he added, before closing his eyes to rest peacefully, "thank you."

"You don't need to thank me," Vaughn said. "We've known each other a long time now, Jack. What are old friends for?"

CHAPTER 19

LOS ANGELES
A FEW DAYS LATER

"Shall we go, then?"

The whirlwind of events in the last few days had finally caught up with Keiko. Her eyes had drifted through the glass walls of Sloane's office, where she sat next to a handsome and crisply dressed CIA agent and across from a stony Arvin Sloane. Out in the hallway, she'd caught sight of her husband, being led out of the APO offices in handcuffs with two armed guards at his side, and for the moment her thoughts were clearly elsewhere. But when Agent Kalt suggested they go, she snapped back to attention.

"Oh! Yes, let's go. But . . ." She glanced back out at Franklin, then looked apologetically at Agent Kalt. "Could I have just a minute first?" The agent nodded patiently, and Keiko stood and strode purposefully out.

"I appreciate your escorting Ms. Thornhill to Washington, Michael," Sloane said after she'd departed, as he leaned arrogantly back at his desk. "Anything you can do to make her debriefing quick and relatively painless would be much appreciated."

"Of course," Agent Kalt replied. "It should be a fairly simple matter. But she's also expressed interest in attending some preliminary agent training briefings at Langley while she's there. Apparently, she has a friend here who thinks she'd be good at the job, and from what I hear, Keiko has the makings of a fine spy."

Sloane considered this with a shrug. "I'll admit, her performance in these very halls just a few days ago would indicate she has the raw skills. She's proven to be quick on her feet, resourceful when necessary, and promising when she's had to adopt alternate personae. With the right guidance—"

"I agree," interrupted Agent Kalt. "I wouldn't be surprised if she were back here before long, drawing a paycheck rather than just visiting."

Sloane's eyebrow cocked up, then he nodded. "Neither would I." With a creepily paternalistic leer, he looked out at Keiko, who was standing very close to her husband in the hallway, speaking softly into Franklin's ear. He was vaguely curious about what she was whispering.

"I read the reports based on your interrogation," Keiko was saying. "And I wanted to tell you that I know why you did what you did."

Franklin seemed humbled, as if the cuffs and the days since Keiko had last seen him had made him smaller somehow. "I loved you, you know," he said pathetically. "I still do."

Keiko said nothing in response. She just placed her hand on his chest, looked him in the eye, and smiled sadly. Then she stepped back, straightened her clothes nervously, and bit her lip. "I believe you," she finally found it in herself to say. Then she turned her back on him, speaking over her shoulder as she walked away: "He's all yours, guys. Thanks."

Franklin looked dumbfounded as the guards

exchanged glances, then prodded him on down the hall. The look of astonishment wouldn't leave Franklin's face all the way out to the truck that would take him to the prison, nor would it have completely vanished even by the time he was tried and sentenced. In fact, it would return to his face regularly, every time he thought of his wife, for the rest of his life. He would never quite understand, and if he ever thought about it, he might realize that something in that lack of comprehension gave the lie to his insistence that he loved her.

For her part, Keiko was about to walk back into Sloane's office when she made a quick detour to a nearby desk. "Tracy?" The junior agent turned from her computer and seemed surprised that Keiko was talking to her. Keiko leaned in to speak conspiratorially. "Could you return this to your boyfriend for me?" Tracy looked confused as Keiko pulled Mark's access card out of her pocket. Then she laughed.

"Mark Baker, you mean?" Tracy succumbed to a mischievous smile as she picked up the card and turned it absently in her hands. "He won't be in today, actually. Let's just say he thinks he's been sent on an important mission to Katmandu. He's in for quite the surprise when he gets there too. I think he'll be careful where he leaves his office supplies next time."

Keiko's smile melted. She fake-laughed politely, as if she understood the joke that Tracy was chuckling darkly about. "Well, tell him I said thanks."

"Will do!" Tracy said brightly, as Keiko shook off her confusion and returned to Sloane's door. Agent Kalt was waiting for her there.

"The plane leaves shortly, Ms. Thornhill."

"It's Ms. Terajima, thank you. From now on. And I'm all ready now, Agent Kalt. I appreciate your patience."

"Call me Mike."

Keiko smiled and put her hand on his arm as he began to escort her out. "You know, I will. I'm looking forward to getting to know you better on the long flight to Washington, Mike. First things first: You have to tell me whether you're seeing anyone, because I think I could find you the perfect girl if you gave me half a chance."

Agent Kalt seemed surprised, then decided to try to turn the conversation towards safer topics. "No, no," he insisted as they disappeared down the tunnel that led out of the APO complex. "What I really want to talk about is how you pulled off such deft spy work without any training."

"Well, everything I know, I learned from Sydney Bristow," Keiko could be heard saying, her voice full of light. "And I'm sure she'd be the first to tell you that it's all about shifting smoothly."

CHAPTER 20

THAT AFTERNOON
LOS ANGELES

The outdoor café was full of men surrounded by their children, celebrating Father's Day with a sunny lunch near the beach. Waiters and waitresses flitted about between tables, bearing plates and glasses, relishing the generous tips of customers flushed with familial happiness. Many of the men sported what were obviously brand-new neckties, and lots of father/child pairs posed for snapshots taken by cooperative busboys. The feeling in the air was festive; Father's Day often brings out the best in people.

Sydney and Jack sat at a corner table, the remnants of brunch on the plates before them and a small but neatly wrapped gift with a big purple bow perched on a chair nearby. Sydney set down her fork, and Jack nodded his head toward the present.

"So," he said, "I can open this now?" Sydney nodded. "It seems to me," Jack muttered as he stripped off the ribbon methodically and opened up the box, "that it's *my* day. I should have been able to open my present whenever I wanted."

"Quit complaining," Sydney replied, laughing. "I thought you should wait until after we'd eaten. You always made me wait for my birthday presents until after dinner when I was growing up."

Jack didn't reply. He had fallen silent when he saw what was in the box. Then the corners of his mouth turned up ever so slightly: the Jack Bristow equivalent of breaking into a huge, pleased grin. "I love it, Sydney. Thank you."

"I'm glad, Dad," Sydney said, leaning over to get another look at it herself. It was a framed photo, lifted from the surveillance cameras in the Gobi facility, that showed Jack fending off the guards as Sydney, in the background, placed a perfect kick into the face of a menacing thug. "I figure you can put it on your desk. The family that kicks butt together, you know . . . Dixon helped me find exactly the right frame. I think it came out nicely."

"The next time I see Dixon I'll have to compliment him," Jack said.

Sydney was pleased. "He'll be so glad you like it. So will Weiss. He helped me crop it. I'd call him up right now to tell him how much you like it, but he and Nadia are out looking for an apartment to move into together. Isn't it sweet that the first thing Eric did when he saw Nadia after the mission was beg her to move in with him? He was so nervous about it before, but then it was all he could talk about. I guess a near-death experience changes you."

"Wait till he has a few more of them," Jack said dryly, sipping at his drink.

Sydney set her napkin down on the table and stood up. "But I told Michael I'd call him to make plans for the afternoon. Do you mind if I step away?"

Jack waved his consent, and Sydney strolled out to the sidewalk to dial Vaughn's number away from the crowd. To her surprise, however, it rang and it rang, but he didn't pick up. Finally Sydney gave up, snapped her phone shut, and headed back into the restaurant to rejoin her father.

* * *

In the dark basement where Vaughn had gone so he wouldn't be overheard, the insistent beep of the call waiting pierced the silence that had fallen when he'd been put on hold. He pulled his phone away from his ear and glanced at the caller ID.

I'm sorry, Syd, he thought to himself sadly. *I promise I'll call you back once this is finished. If it's ever finished, that is. . . .*

He waited a moment more, drumming his fingers on the damp wall and looking over his shoulder now and then guiltily, until finally a voice came on the other end of the line.

"Is this Michael Vaughn?"

"Yes, it is," Vaughn responded tensely, hunching unconsciously to make it even less likely anyone could hear him. "I was told I could reach you here."

"It's been a long time."

"Yes. Yes, it has. Listen, some photos I took six years ago came up in an investigation recently, and I need to be sure nothing else I gave you back then could appear in the future."

"Michael," said Arnold Paulson silkily, "I'm sure we could work out some sort of quid pro quo for the rest of your reconnaissance files, if you like."

Vaughn was silent, unhappy.

"Surely, old friend, you didn't expect me to return everything to you and receive nothing in return?" Paulson said, delighted in having the upper hand.

Vaughn clenched his fist. *Maybe I should just tell Sydney all about this,* he thought in frustration. *But when?*

ABOUT THE AUTHOR

Steven Hanna is a freelance writer who lives in Los Angeles.